SHARP SHOT

JACK HIGGINS

WITH JUSTIN RICHARDS

SHARP SHOT

HarperCollins *Children's Books*

First published in paperback in Great Britain by
HarperCollins *Children's Books* 2009

HarperCollins *Children's Books* is a division of HarperCollins*Publishers* Ltd
77-85 Fulham Palace Road, Hammersmith, London W6 8JB

Visit us on the web at www.harpercollins.co.uk

1

Printed and bound in England by Clays Ltd, St Ives plc

Jack Higgins lived in Belfast till the age of twelve. Leaving school at fifteen, he spent three years with the Royal Horse Guards, serving on the East German border during the Cold War. His subsequent employment included occupations as diverse as circus roustabout, truck driver, clerk, teacher and university lecturer. *The Eagle has Landed* turned him into an international bestselling author, and his novels have since sold over 250 million copies and have been translated into fifty-five languages.

Justin Richards is the is the author of dozens of books, including many *Doctor Who* novels, *The Death Collector* and his *Agent Alfie* series for younger readers. He worked in the computer industry before moving into full-time writing and editing and has also written for the stage and the screen.

Prologue

1990. Southern Iraq.

John Chance raised his powerful binoculars and focused on the low building on the other side of the sand dune. It was an Iraqi nuclear lab, and according to British Intelligence, it was close to producing a viable bomb. According to Saddam Hussein, on the other hand, Iraq had no nuclear weapons programme – and this secret lab in the desert simply didn't exist.

It was John Chance's job to make sure that by the end of the day, it really didn't.

"You think they've got nukes in there?" asked Dex Halford. He was Chance's number two on this mission, a wiry but powerful man with dark hair. At that moment his hair was covered by a brown headscarf. Like the long cloak he wore over his uniform, it was designed to blend in with the sand of the desert, and to give the impression at a distance that he was a local tribesman.

"Too soon," said Chance. "The assessment from MI6 says they've only just got the place up and running. They may have some raw material, but it's unlikely they'll have anything weapons-grade yet."

"Not impossible, though. Six have been wrong before," said Ferdy McCain. He was the shortest of the team, stocky and heavy set. A thin, dark moustache made him look more like an Italian gangster than an elite British Special Forces operative.

"There was a rumour they got stuff out of the Al-Maan facility before Mossad, the Israeli counter terrorism unit, paid it a visit," said Halford. "If they did, they'll have brought it here."

Any further discussion was interrupted by the fourth member of the team. "We've got company," called Mark Darrow from the other side of the shallow dip where they were hiding.

Chance signalled for McCain and Halford to stay where they were, and crawled over to have a look.

Darrow was on the other side of the Jeep – a camouflage net had been spread over the vehicle and staked with tent pegs to keep it in place. The back of the Jeep was stacked with equipment, including several boxes of high explosives.

"What is it?" asked Chance, lying flat beside Darrow so that only his scarf-wrapped head poked above the rise of the dune.

Darrow pointed into the distance, and Chance raised his binoculars. A long way off, but heading towards them, he could see a line of camels. The image shimmered in the heat, but even at this distance Chance could see the Bedouin tribes people walking alongside. He smiled grimly as he saw that one of the camels had a baby camel strapped to its back – so the infant wouldn't slow them down.

"They might go right past," said Darrow. "But evening will be drawing in soon, and they'll want to set up camp before it gets cold. They must know the plant is there, I reckon they'll use the buildings for shelter from the night wind. They'll know the weather's due to break any time."

"And if they do pitch camp close to the nuclear facility…"

"It'll keep some of the Republican Guards busy watching them, and maybe they'll take the blame," Darrow finished for him. "Good diversion."

But that wasn't what Chance had in mind. "If they camp too close, they'll be caught in the blast. That place will go with one hell of a bang."

"We'll make sure of it." Darrow grinned. "And if they find a few Bedouin bodies in the wreckage, all the better."

Chance looked at him coldly. "We've got an hour before we need to get ready. You stay here with Halford." He turned and called across to the other two men. "Dex, stay here with Darrow. Ferdy – you're with me."

"Where are we going?" asked Ferdy McCain as he hurried over to join Chance.

"We're going to warn those Bedouin that they need to camp somewhere else."

"You're crazy," Darrow told him. "They don't owe us anything – what if they chop you down where you stand?"

Chance fixed him with a piercing stare. "We're surgeons not butchers," he said quietly. "We're here to save lives, not to take them. Yes, there will be some casualties, but no more than necessary. Our target is that nuclear facility and whatever they have there. Not the guards, though we'll take them out if we have to. Not the scientists, who are probably working under duress anyway, but again, we'll take them out if we must. But there is no excuse – *no* excuse – for putting innocent lives in danger unless we absolutely have to. Got that?"

Darrow turned away.

Chance grabbed his shoulder and turned him back. "You got that?" he repeated.

"I got that," Darrow told him, eyes hard and expression set. "And I have to tell you, *sir*, if that's your attitude, you'll never get far in this job."

"If that's *your* attitude," Chance replied calmly, "then you're in the *wrong* job." He turned to McCain. "You fit?"

"Ready when you are, boss."

"Then let's save some lives." Chance glanced at Darrow before adding: "Because ultimately, *that's* our job."

The temperature fell sharply at night, but John Chance didn't feel the cold. His entire focus was on the job in hand. Halford and Darrow had set up a mass of squibs and explosives on the far side of the Iraqi installation. The explosives would go off like grenades, while the squibs simulated gunfire.

"All set?" asked Chance, as Halford returned.

They had left their cloaks in the Jeep, though they still wore their headscarves. The wind was getting up and sand whipped at their faces. The promised sandstorm wouldn't be long in coming.

Halford was nodding. "Going to be a hell of a fireworks show."

"Just so long as it draws out the Republican Guards so we can get inside and mine the building."

"And the scientists and civilian workers?"

"Tell them to run for it. Brought your phrasebook?"

Halford brandished his assault rifle. "I think I can communicate with them. They'll know to run. You get on all right with those Bedouin, by the way?"

Chance grinned. "I managed to get the message across. They've moved on, so I think they understood."

"They might have said thank you," Halford told him.

"They did. The head man's a guy called Kassim. He gave me a baby camel."

"You what?!" Halford looked round, as if expecting to see a small camel join them on the mission.

Chance grinned. "It's all right. I asked him to look after it for me till I can come back and collect it."

After another hour, the wind had picked up and the sand was swirling. Chance decided it was time to make their move. If they waited any longer the sandstorm would be too intense for them to get away.

On Chance's signal, Halford set off the diversionary explosions and squibs. The desert erupted with sound and fury. Flashes illuminated frozen images of the swirling sand like photographs. Gunfire seemed to rip through the northern side of the installation.

Immediately there was answering fire from the Iraqi guards. An armoured car positioned outside the main gates lurched into life and rumbled round to the back of the perimeter wall to engage the apparent attack.

With the main gates now only guarded by a few nervous soldiers, the SAS team made their move. Silent and swift, shadows in the night, they took down the guards. Chance knocked out two of the soldiers. Halford slammed another into the wall of the guardhouse, where he collapsed unconscious. McCain dealt swiftly with a guard who'd managed to draw his gun, but had no time to fire before McCain's knife sliced into his leg. Moments later the guard was gagged and bound, his leg strapped up and bandaged to staunch the bleeding.

Only Darrow had to kill. His automatic rifle, fitted with a silencer, took out three guards on duty on the high perimeter wall. Two dropped where they were standing. The third pitched forwards, falling without making a sound to crunch on the ground at Darrow's feet. He smiled with cold satisfaction.

Chance's whispered instructions were loud and clear in the earphones of his team. "We have access. Time to go to your positions. Ferdy, maintain surveillance and let us know if the guards realise they've been conned. Dex, you take the guardhouse and the watch towers. Mark, you've got the offices and admin complex as we agreed. I'll deal with the main lab. Set the charges to blow in twenty minutes from my mark, and make sure you're back at the Jeep by then. OK?"

After each of his men had checked in, Chance told them: "Right then. Ten minutes from... Now. Go go go!"

They moved swiftly and silently through the complex. Like so much of Saddam's weapons programme, the design for the plant was stolen. Chance had studied the plans of the Russian installation it was based on. He knew exactly where the main lab would be, and the quickest, safest route to get there.

He didn't see anyone on his journey through the dimly lit corridors until he was almost at his destination. Then he pressed himself into an alcove to allow a white-coated scientist to pass. The man was carrying something – Chance got only a glimpse, but it was obviously heavy and it seemed to be made of stone. A statue, maybe, about half a metre tall... The scientist looked worried and anxious as he hurried past.

As soon as the corridor was clear, Chance ran quickly to the security door at the end. There was a numbered keypad beside the heavy, lead-lined door. Chance didn't waste time trying to work out the code. The door might be strong and the lock might be unbreakable. But the hinges were a weak point.

Chance took what looked like an oversized tube of toothpaste from his backpack. He squeezed thick grey paste from it, like bathroom sealant, down the edge of the door and over the hinges. Finally, he stuck a small metal pin into the grey paste. The end of the pin glowed red.

Hurrying back to the alcove, Chance pulled out a small plastic box with a switch on it. He turned away, and pressed the switch.

The sound of the explosion echoed down the corridor, followed immediately by a cloud of smoke. As the sound and smoke cleared, the high-pitched wail of an alarm kicked in.

The door was lying sideways on the ground. Chance jumped over it as he ran into the main laboratory. Several technicians and scientists were cowering in a corner in fright. Chance spared them a brief glance.

"Are you paying attention?" he shouted in the local dialect above the sound of the alarm.

"Yes," one of the scientists replied in a quivering voice.

"Good. Make sure you take the guard trussed up in the gatehouse with you, he'll have trouble walking on his own. And then you've got ten minutes to get the hell out of here before the whole place goes up." Chance was kneeling on the ground, backpack on the floor in front of him, pulling objects from it. He held one up – you didn't need to be an expert to guess that the stubby brown cylinder was an explosive.

"So, what are you waiting for?" said Chance, positioning the first of the high explosive charges against a bank of computer servers. He checked his watch and set the timer.

When he looked back over his shoulder, the lab was empty.

Five minutes later, Chance had set explosives at key points around the room. He made sure the vital areas would take the brunt of the blasts: the containment vessels, the centrifuges, the data storage... He took the empty backpack with him – there was no point in leaving behind anything that might identify who had been there. The main reason for using Chance and his team rather than an airstrike was that no one would know for sure who had destroyed the place.

With the alarms going, the Republican Guards would be hurrying back from the diversion Halford and Darrow had arranged. Assault rifle at the ready and set to deliver continuous automatic fire, Chance ran from the laboratory.

He had to assume anyone he saw would be hostile. The civilians should be running for their lives. He knew from the regular location and progress updates in his earpiece exactly where all the members of his own team were. Anyone coming back into the facility had to be the enemy. Chance cut down three soldiers in the corridor – taking them out before they even knew he was there.

Out into the central compound Chance hurled several smoke canisters. It would slow down the returning troops, and it would mask his own escape. A dark shape passed him in the fog of yellow smoke, and Chance shouted at it:

"The lab is secure," he yelled in the local dialect. "The problem is in the admin block." He smiled grimly as he heard his words repeated by the incoming soldiers.

A bullet meant for Chance ricocheted off the wall close to the main gate. He turned and fired on instinct and a khaki-clad figure collapsed behind him. Chance didn't wait to see if any others followed. He was running across the sand, away from the noise and confusion, away from the smoke and the bullets. A quick look at his watch told him there was no time to hang around.

He reached the sand dune and hurled himself over, rolling down the other side and skidding to a halt close to the Jeep.

Dex Halford looked down at him from where he was sitting nonchalantly in the driver's seat. The door was open and he was dangling his legs over the side, swigging from his water bottle.

"What kept you?" Dex asked with a grin.

McCain was in the passenger seat. "If you're late you ride in the back," he called. Then he frowned. "Isn't Darrow with you?"

"He's cutting it fine," said Chance, checking his watch. The second hand was sweeping up towards the 12. Just a few seconds. "Five," he muttered as he counted them off. "Four... three..."

"Here he comes," said Halford.

A dark shape rolled down the dune, just as Chance himself had done. "Sorry I'm late," said Darrow as he reached the Jeep.

If he said anything else, it was lost in the sound of the blast. The night sky was turned to sudden daylight. Brilliant yellow washed across the landscape and a ball of smoke and fire mushroomed upwards.

"Time we were going," said Chance as the noise

died away. "You and I get to ride in the back," he told Darrow, slapping his comrade on the shoulder.

"Chauffeur service, I love it." Darrow swung his backpack off and dragged it up into the Jeep with him.

Chance watched him, puzzled. The backpack was obviously heavy – very heavy. But it should have been empty.

The Jeep bumped over the rise and tipped down the other side of the dune, gathering speed. In the distance, the installation was burning. Tiny figures – soldiers, civilians and scientists – were milling round it in confusion.

"Job done," McCain called from the front of the Jeep.

"Nice one, team," Chance told them. "Just two small loose ends to tie up, then we're home and dry."

"And what are those?" Darrow asked.

"First," Chance told him, "there's the small matter of the team photograph. And second – I want to know what you've got in your rucksack."

Darrow met Chance's gaze. For a moment he said nothing. Then he looked away. "Souvenir. I'll show you when it gets light."

The plan was to cross the border into East Araby, a small country to the south east of Iraq, also bordering Kuwait and Saudi Arabia. By daybreak, Chance's team was within a hundred and fifty kilometres of the border. In the Jeep, it would take only a few more hours.

They heard the plane long before they saw it.

"One of ours?" Darrow wondered.

"Doubt it," said Halford. "We need to find some cover."

"Camouflage netting?" McCain suggested.

Chance shook his head. "We have to assume they're looking for us. We'll need better cover than that." He had the map open on his knees. "Head slightly to the left, over that rise. There should be the remains of a village."

A small black shape skimmed the horizon over to their right. The plane turned slowly, heading back towards them.

"Has it seen us?" Darrow wondered.

"Not yet," Chance shouted above the roar of the Jeep as Halford accelerated. "Might see the sand we're kicking up, but we'll have to risk that."

McCain had his binoculars out. "Iraqi air force markings. It's a Foxbat."

Chance swore. The MiG25 – codenamed *Foxbat* by NATO forces – was a powerful aircraft. It was fast enough to outrun an air-to-air missile, but the good news was that it didn't carry ground-attack weapons. It was used for reconnaissance and interception only. Banking steeply, it disappeared into the distance.

Ahead of them were the remains of the village. It was more like a small town – derelict stone-built structures disappearing into the distance. Most of the roofs had collapsed, some buildings reduced to just a couple of broken walls.

"You could get lost in there for a week," said McCain.

Halford steered the Jeep rapidly between several low walls, then over a bank of sand and into the enclosed remains of a house. The Jeep jolted to a stop, and immediately Darrow and Chance were unrolling the camouflage netting and dragging it over the vehicle.

All four of them were out of the building in moments, taking shelter in the shadow of a section of wall thirty metres away. If the Foxbat returned, it was more likely to spot the Jeep. If it did, they wanted to be far away from it.

"Can't hear anything," said McCain. "Maybe we're OK?"

"Give it half an hour," Chance decided. "It may have spotted us and called in support. We don't want to be caught in the open if it comes back, especially if he's got company."

"Time for the team photo then," Halford decided. He took out a disposable camera. The camera had come from a supermarket, but Halford had removed the cardboard casing that gave away its origins. It was plain, functional, black plastic.

"Right," said Halford, "the challenge is to work out how we take a picture with us all in. There's no timer."

McCain sighed and took the camera. "Why do I always have to be the practical one? I need a small stone about... this big." He held his thumb and forefinger in a small circle.

There was no shortage of stones about the right size – just big enough to cover the camera's shutter button. McCain balanced the camera on a low section of wall that protruded from a higher wall. Then he put heavy stones round the camera to hold it in place. He wedged another on the top, jutting out over the lens, but leaving the shutter button with the small stone on it exposed.

"Right, assume your positions."

"Is that it?" Halford asked, laughing. "Now what?"

"Yeah," said Darrow, "what's the big deal. Someone still needs to press the shutter."

"I think that's the idea," said Chance. "Right, Ferdy?"

McCain was grinning. "Exactly right. Get ready. The camera's lined up with this bit of wall here, so let's all stand in front of it. Oh, and we'll need some pebbles. About this big, I should think." He picked up a stone the size of an egg and weighed it in his hand. "Yes, that should do it. I'll go first."

"What are you going to do?" Darrow asked.

"Bung rocks at it. Ready?"

They could see at once what McCain meant when he tossed the egg-sized stone. He lobbed it up on to higher section of wall. The stone rattled down the wall, bouncing on to the stones holding the camera steady.

"Missed," said McCain. "Who's going next?"

The third pebble did it. Halford arced it into the air above the wall just as first McCain and then Darrow had done. The pebble rattled down, and this time struck the small stone on the shutter button. The weight of the impact was enough to take the picture.

"Nice one, Ferdy," said Chance as they all watched

him retrieve the camera and wind on the film. "Now then, let's see what Mark's got in his backpack, shall we?"

Reluctantly, Darrow opened his rucksack and lifted out his 'souvenir'. It was a statue made from a dark brown material, like terracotta, about half a metre tall and maybe fifteen centimetres wide. It was in the shape of a lion standing upright on its back legs, and it was obviously old; the features and details had worn away, the material scuffed and scratched and flaking. Chance remembered that one of the scientists had been carrying it – he must have run into Darrow soon after.

"Blimey, it's heavy," McCain commented, lifting it up to get a better look. "What d'you want this for?"

"It just took my fancy." Darrow lifted the statue carefully out of McCain's hands and pushed it back into his rucksack. "No big deal."

"Reckon it's valuable?" Halford asked.

"I'll let you know."

Chance was looking grim. "You shouldn't have taken it," he said. "We didn't come here to steal artefacts, whether they're valuable or not."

"Oh come on, John," said Darrow, suddenly angry. "We were going to blow it up. I found it in the admin block when I was planting the explosives. It just seemed a shame to destroy it. So where's the harm? I mean, they're not going to come and ask for it back, are they?"

"Actually," said Halford, "I think they might." He pointed across the mass of broken buildings and collapsed walls.

Two small black shapes were streaking rapidly towards them across the sky. As they watched, one of the black shapes flashed, as if it had caught the sun.

"Incoming!" yelled McCain.

Moments later, a building just thirty metres away exploded in a fireball. Heavy machine gun fire strafed across the sandy ground.

The four men hurled themselves into the cover of the wall. There was another explosion, even closer. A wall exploded under the impact of the rocket, stone and debris flying through the air. Darrow gave a cry as a lump of rock struck him across the side of the head, hurling him sideways.

Then as suddenly as it had started, the attack stopped. The two aircraft sped onwards, into the distance.

"Soon as they turn, they'll be back," said Halford.

Chance was beside the prone body of Darrow. "Out cold. He's losing blood, and I think his collar bone's broken. We have to get him to the Jeep."

"That could be a problem," said McCain, kneeling beside them. He pointed across to the burning remains of the building that had taken the first rocket hit. "That's the Jeep. Maybe they saw its heat signature."

"Then we have to walk. We'll take it in turns to carry Mark. We move out as soon as it's safe."

"And when will that be?"

"The planes aren't turning," Halford reported, joining them. "I reckon the Foxbat wasn't sure he'd seen anything, and they were just making sure, maybe trying to flush us out if we were here. They fired at anything showing up on the infra red and just got lucky.""And we didn't," said Chance. "They might send in ground forces to check. Let's make sure there's nothing left of the Jeep, and we bury anything that we don't take with us. We need to travel light. With luck we can call in an extraction, but if not then it's still another hundred and fifty kilometres to the border. So the only thing we're taking with us apart from water and weapons and the first aid kit is Mark, got it?"

"What about this?" McCain asked, kicking Darrow's

heavy rucksack containing his souvenir statue.

"You check on the Jeep," Chance told him. "Dex, you do what you can to help Mark. See if you can stop the bleeding." He picked up the rucksack – it really was very heavy, and there was no way they could take it with them and carry Darrow. Speed was vital now. "I'll bury this with the rest of the gear," he said.

1

The present day. Gloucestershire, England.

Jade Chance was out jogging. The route she took –
through the village and back across the hills – was
almost exactly six and a half kilometres. She tried to
run every day after school, and occasionally she
persuaded her brother Rich to go with her.

But not this afternoon.

When he was at home, Dad quite often joined her.
Jade had expected him to be slow and out of condition.
He ate the most appalling rubbish, he smoked –
though less than he used to – and as far as Jade could
tell he drank only black coffee, beer and champagne.
Sometimes together.

It was November, so it was already dark when Jade
got back. She'd left Rich doing his homework, and

he was still at it when she returned.

"Dad phoned," said Rich, without looking up. He was sitting at the dining table in the main living room of the small cottage the three of them shared on the outskirts of the small Cotswold village.

"Did he say where he is or what he's doing?" Jade asked, going straight through to the kitchen.

"Nope."

"Did he say when he'll be back?" Jade called as she opened the fridge.

"Nope."

"Did he say where he's put the tin opener?"

"Nope," Rich called back. "But I did ask," he added after a moment.

"Liar." Jade started to unload the beer and champagne from the fridge. "So why did he bother to call?"

"Don't know. That was something I *didn't* ask." Rich was standing in the doorway, watching Jade empty the fridge. "I hope you're not going to empty all that down the sink again," he said.

"No. But I don't see why the fridge has to be full of Dad's booze. One bottle of champagne and two bottles of beer, that's what he's allowed now. If you've finished your homework, you can go online and order some real food and drink."

"You mean healthy stuff." Rich was smiling. "You mean lettuce and carrots and things that only rabbits eat. You mean fruit juice and bottled water."

"Among other things." Jade stood up and surveyed the collection of bottles on the worktop. "That should do it. If we're left on our own to look after ourselves, we might as well eat healthily and sensibly while we can. He could be gone for weeks. Are you sure he didn't say when he'll be back?"

Rich shrugged. "He's working for Ardman. He could be anywhere in the world for days or weeks or even months, I guess."

"All the more reason to make the most of it."

"Yeah," Rich agreed. "I did an order yesterday, anyway. They're supposed to deliver it this evening. Don't worry, I put us down for some health food. Salad and fruit and vegetables. Oh, and I ordered some Coke and burgers too. And we can have pizza tonight." He grinned at Jade's horrified expression. "You can put extra pineapple on yours. Then it'll count as fruit."

Before Jade could protest, her phone beeped. It was warning her it was almost out of power, so she went through to her bedroom to plug it into the charger. By the time she returned, Rich was back at his homework.

There was something else Jade was determined to do while Dad was away. That was to unpack at least some of the crates and boxes that had been standing unopened in the spare room since they'd arrived several months earlier.

Dad was used to living out of suitcases and boxes, but since the death of the twins' mother, Jade hadn't really felt anywhere was home. If she unpacked Dad's stuff, if they filled the cottage with things that belonged to them as a family rather than the people they were renting the cottage from, then maybe this would become home.

It frustrated Jade that Rich didn't seem to have the same problem. Maybe he was more like their dad. He seemed happy just to unpack things as and when – and if – he needed them. If she left it to the men, Jade knew, they'd never be moved in.

Another reason for unpacking, though she could barely admit it to herself, was that despite everything Jade was enjoying her new life. Dad could be annoying and irritating, but he'd demonstrated time and again the lengths he'd go to for his children. It was strange to think that less than a year ago John Chance hadn't even known he *had* children, and they'd known nothing about him…

School was OK, and Jade had made some friends. There was a time, a few months back, when she'd expected to be asked to leave. But Dad's boss Ardman had somehow persuaded the Head and Governors that getting involved in an armed siege during which large sections of the school were blown up, and others demolished by various members of the Chance family – including Dad, who'd driven his BMW right through the main reception block – wasn't actually an expellable offence.

Somewhere at the back of Jade's mind was the thought that if she got everything unpacked, it would be that much more difficult, that much more unlikely, that they would have to move on. The cottage might not seem quite like home yet, but she hoped it soon would.

"Box time!" she called to Rich as she packed the beer and champagne into a cupboard.

"What, again?"

"One a day, remember? We agreed." She went back

through to the living room.

"We didn't agree," Rich told her. "You decided. An agreement requires the consent of both parties."

Jade sighed, deciding it wasn't worth an argument. "You sort out the shopping," she said. "I'll do the box after I've had a shower. Deal?"

"I suppose."

Jade grinned. Her twin brother drove her every bit as mad as her dad did. But she couldn't imagine being without him. She went into the bathroom, thinking how lucky she was really to have Dad and Rich. How lucky she was that no one had tried to kill her for months now.

But that was about to change.

Rich watched as Jade dragged a large cardboard box in from the spare room. She sat cross-legged on the floor beside it. Her shoulder-length fair hair was still wet, and she'd pulled on a sweat shirt and jogging bottoms.

"Anything good?" Rich asked.

"Books, papers, magazines." Jade pulled out a handful of magazines and spread them on the carpet beside her. "I mean, why does he keep this stuff?"

"You can always put it away again."

She was leafing through the different magazines – *National Geographic, The Rifleman, The Economist, History Today, Jane's Intelligence Review...* The books were just as varied. There was a battered hardback copy of *Oliver Twist* stacked with a book about the Falklands War. Jade pulled out a paperback thriller published in the 1970s. The cover was a photograph of a woman dressed in combat uniform. Or rather, half dressed in it. Jade tossed it to one side.

"That looks good," said Rich, kneeling down beside her.

"No it doesn't," she told him. "Leave it where it is. That's the rubbish pile."

"Dad might want to read it again."

"You think he got past the front cover the first time?" Jade threw another paperback after it, it landed face down.

"What was that one?" Rich asked eagerly.

"You don't want to know."

"You mean *you* don't want me to know."

Jade had lifted out another stack of books and magazines. There was an old newspaper on the top. The headline read, 'Government Denies SAS Involvement in Hostage Rescue'. Underneath it was another paper – a lurid tabloid from the same day. Its headline was: 'Our Boys Give 'Em Hell'.

"Wonder why he's kept these?" said Rich.

"Like we can't guess."

"Shall I put them with the photos?"

Jade nodded. "Good idea."

There was a small desk in the corner of the room, by the French doors. These opened on to a small patio overlooking the back garden. The desk had a sloping front that folded down to become a writing area. Behind it was a rack of pigeon holes and compartments. Jade had found a stack of old photos in one of Dad's boxes, and put them inside the desk. Since then they had found several more to add to the collection.

The newspapers were too big to go with the photos, so Rich put them in an empty drawer in the bottom part of the desk. Jade seemed busy unpacking the box, so Rich opened the lid of the desk and took out the bundle of photographs.

There were maybe twenty or so, taken at different times in different places. Most of them showed John Chance – in army dress uniform, in a dinner suit, on an assault course covered in mud, but grinning. There was a crumpled picture of Rich and Jade's mother. It was a small, creased, passport-sized shot, and it looked like it had been kept in a wallet or a pocket for years.

But the picture that intrigued Rich was a faded snapshot taken in the desert. At least, it looked like the desert – there was lots of sand, but the four men in it were standing in front of a low wall. All four were dressed in khaki army uniforms. One of them was a younger John Chance, another Rich and Jade knew was Dex Halford, who'd been in the SAS with their dad. They both looked so young – in their mid-twenties, Rich guessed.

One of the other two men was slightly shorter and stocky with a thin, dark moustache. He was standing beside John Chance, looking slightly wary. The fourth man was wiry and had a shock of hair the same colour as the sand. He was grinning and pointing at the camera with one hand, while his other hand was resting on Dex Halford's shoulder.

On the back of the photo was written in biro: *Iraq – November 1990. JC, DH, Mark and Ferdy.*

"What's that noise?" Jade asked suddenly.

Rich pushed the photos back inside the desk,

dropped the newspapers in front of them, and closed the lid. "I didn't hear anything."

"Sounded like thunder."

Rich pulled out his mobile phone. "I'll check the forecast." He started up the web browser. It drained the battery, but he enjoyed using it.

"Gadget man," said Jade. "Why don't you just look outside?"

"It's dark," Rich protested as he waited for the webpage to load.

"You can still tell if it's raining. Rain – you know, that wet stuff that drops from the sky."

"Nothing forecast," Rich told her.

He pushed his phone back into his pocket and opened the French doors. The evening was quite warm for late autumn. There was a half moon and the sky looked clear. Rich stepped out on to the patio. The security light on the wall above came on at once, detecting Rich's movement as he walked.

The small garden ended with a wooden fence made of thin panels. There was a gate that led out to the small wooded area beyond. Behind that were fields and a small stream snaking through the hills. To Rich, brought up in an American city before the twins' mother brought them home to Britain, it seemed very isolated and quiet.

Now the quiet was shattered by the sound Jade had mistaken for thunder. Standing outside, Rich could hear it much more clearly. It was coming from the woods behind the house.

It was gunfire.

Rich stepped quickly back inside and locked the French doors.

Outside, the security light went off. The doors were reflective panels of black. Rich found himself looking at his own reflection, Jade standing beside him.

"Fireworks, do you think?" said Jade.

"No. Guns."

Typical, thought Jade. *Just when it seemed like we could finally settle down...*

"Might just be hunters," she said, hopefully.

"At night?"

Jade sighed. "OK, we'd better take cover. And call the police."

At that moment the security light came on again, bathing the patio in harsh white light.

Rich and Jade took a step backwards, as a dark shape approached the cottage. It crashed into the doors, bursting them open. A man staggered into the room, his eyes wide and staring. His face was caked in blood and his clothes were tattered and dirty.

Rich stared open mouthed. He knew the man. He'd been looking at his picture just now. He might be twenty years older, his sandy hair going grey, but it was obviously one of the men from the photograph taken in Iraq.

"Chance!" the man gasped. "Looking for John Chance. He's the only person who can help me now." The man collapsed to his knees, then toppled forwards to fall motionless at Rich's feet.

2

"He's still breathing," said Jade, kneeling to examine the man. She felt his pulse, and it was strong if a bit fast. Then again, Jade wasn't really sure what was normal.

"He's in that picture," said Rich. "One of Dad's friends from the army. The SAS." He turned out the lights.

"Hey, what did you do that for?" Jade demanded.

"If there's someone else out there with a gun, we don't want them finding us too easily."

The man was coming round. He blinked and shook his head, pulling himself into a sitting position.

"Hey, steady," said Jade. "Rich – get him some water."

Rich hurried to the kitchen and was straight back with a tumbler of tap water. The man accepted it gratefully, though he spilled quite a bit down his muddy shirt. He was shivering despite the fact it was a mild evening, and he was wearing a heavy leather jacket.

"John Chance," he gasped again. "Got to get to John Chance."

Jade nodded. "He's not here. He's away." She glanced at Rich, before adding: "Can we help? I'm Jade and this is Rich – John's our dad."

"Away?" The man looked annoyed as much as frightened. "Why didn't I know?"

"Probably because he's on a secret mission," Rich muttered. "No one is supposed to know."

Jade glared at him. This wasn't the time for criticism. "Can we help?" she asked the man again. "What's the matter? We heard shooting – is someone after you?"

"They'll kill me," the man said. He looked nervously over to the doors. The patio was still lit up by the security light; the door was swinging back and forth in the breeze, its catch broken. "If they find me, they'll kill me. I thought Chance would help. I have to get away from them." He grabbed the sleeve of Jade's sweatshirt. "You have to help me. Get me away from here."

There was a rattle of machine gun fire from somewhere outside – closer than before. Rich hurried to the windows and looked out.

"Can't see anyone, but we have to assume they'll find us. Were they close behind you?"

The man shook his head. "But they'll be here. We have to go. Now!"

Rich nodded. But to Jade's surprise he opened the desk, and hunted through for a photograph.

"This isn't a Kodak moment," she told him. "It's a get the hell out of here moment."

Rich had found what he was looking for. It was a faded photo of four men standing by a wall in the desert. He pointed to one of the men.

"That's Dad. And that's Dex Halford… And that…" He tapped the man standing beside their dad, then pointed to the man sitting on the floor.

Jade took the photo and held it so the man could see. "So, are you Mark or Ferdy?"

The man blinked. "McCain – Ferdy McCain. That was in Iraq, back in 1990 with the Regiment. We took out a secret nuclear facility."

"Hey, cool," said Rich.

"Yeah, OK – in that case you really are a friend of Dad's," said Jade. She gave the photo back to Rich who stuffed it in his pocket. The she helped Ferdy McCain to his feet. "Now, let's get you out of here and call for help."

"Got my phone," said Rich. "We'll do it on the way."

Outside, the security light had gone out. With the lights in the room turned out too, they could see out into the gloom of the garden. Jade was sure she could see movement, down by the fence. "Time to go," she said urgently.

"I'll be all right," McCain assured them. "I've been through worse. Just tired."

Rich led the way out of the dining room and into the hall. The front door had a frosted window set high in it. Through the glass they could see the silhouette of a man's head and shoulders.

The sound of the doorbell was deafeningly loud, and made Jade flinch.

"Gunmen," Rich hissed.

"Who ring the bell?" said Jade. "Yeah, right."

"You're not going to answer it?"

Jade didn't reply. She marched down the hallway and opened the front door. Outside was a man in uniform. He turned towards them and smiled.

"Supermarket delivery. From our shop to your step, guaranteed." His uniform was bright green and he was holding a clipboard. "We didn't have any concentrated vita-mineral supplement drink, I'm afraid."

From the dining room came the sound of breaking glass followed by a shout.

"Don't think we'll be needing it," Jade told the man, and pushed him out of the way.

"Healthy exercise coming up," Rich agreed, as he and McCain ran past.

The supermarket lorry was almost blocking the narrow lane. The delivery man wouldn't be so happy, Jade thought, when he found out he had to back nearly a quarter of a mile before he could turn it round. Quarter of a mile to the main road through the village.

A quarter of a mile they were never going to make. A car was coming. Its lights raked across the hedges either side of the lane as it slewed along having taken the corner too fast. The roar of its engine was louder than the idling of the lorry.

"Not going that way," said Jade.

"What's going on?" the delivery man called. His voice was drowned out by the sound of gunfire from inside the cottage. The dining room window overlooking the lane exploded. Bullets ripped into the tarmac close to where Jade and Rich were standing.

McCain was already running. "Come on!" he yelled, hauling himself up into the cab of the lorry.

"Hey!" the delivery man yelled, running after them.

Jade and Rich were round the other side of the lorry, pulling themselves up into the cab as it started to move off.

"You driven one of these before?" Rich asked as he sat in the middle of the wide bench seat. Next to him, Jade heaved the door shut.

"Not with a freezer compartment stuck on the back," McCain told him. The lorry was picking up speed. The lights from the car behind were approaching rapidly, dazzling in the mirror.

There was a loud bump from the back of the lorry. Jade could see in the wing mirror that plastic crates were falling out of the back, scattering across the road.

"That was your pizza," she told Rich.

The car had to slew and weave to avoid the fallen crates. It was catching them up, but there was no way it could get ahead of them in the narrow lane. The lorry was picking up speed.

Then Jade realised something that made her throat go dry. "Where exactly are we going?" she asked.

Rich worked it out at the same moment. She could see it in his eyes, the way he had gone pale. There was a rattle of gunfire, and the wing mirror crazed. The glass held for a moment, a spider's web criss-crossing it, then it fell away.

"This is a dead end," said Rich. "It doesn't go anywhere – just a gate and field and the brook."

"Now you tell me," Ferdy said. "Still, she's a big powerful beast." He dropped down a gear and the engine roared.

A metal field gate loomed in the headlights. The lorry shuddered as it slammed into it. The gate squealed and ripped free, flying sideways. The lorry lurched, skidded on the muddy field, but kept going down the shallow incline. Sheep scattered.

"A brook won't give it much trouble," said McCain confidently.

" 'The brook' is just a name," Jade told him. "It's a river. A *big* river. And we're heading straight for it!"

The headlights were bouncing as the lorry bumped

across the uneven field. They shimmered on the wide stretch of water beyond the trees ahead. McCain swerved to avoid a tractor parked at the side of the field, before lining up with a gap in the tree line.

What wasn't obvious until they were too close to stop was the drop from the field down to the level of the river. Jade felt the moment the front wheels left the ground. The front of the lorry hung in the air for a moment, then crashed down.

The cab lurched, and the muddy edge of the river rushed towards the windscreen. There was a terrific crunch of metal.

Jade's legs jarred painfully against the dashboard. Instinctively she braced with her hands, just stopping her head from hitting the windscreen. Rich wasn't so lucky – he banged his head hard against the tape deck as the impact threw his body forwards.

The windscreen crazed, then shattered. Water splashed in. The lorry skidded onwards for a few more metres, sagging to one side as the axle gave way. A wheel bounced ahead of them into the water. The sound of metal on mud, then on stones, then on water, was deafening. Steam erupted from the bonnet of the lorry, rising in front of them.

Then one of the headlights went out. Silence. For several seconds all was still.

"You OK?" Jade asked Rich.

He raised his hand to his head, and felt the blood trickling from a miraculously shallow cut. He winced. "Yeah, just about."

"Out – we have to get out!" McCain yelled.

The door beside Jade had buckled and wouldn't move. McCain bent round, braced himself against Rich, and kicked at his door with both feet. It fell from the side of the vehicle and clattered and splashed into the river.

They hauled themselves out. The lights of the pursuing car were sweeping across the field above and behind them.

"What now?" Rich wondered.

"Sorry, guys," said McCain. "We might have to swim for it. But I'm afraid we'll be sitting ducks."

"Swimming ducks," said Rich. "Ducks don't sit on the water. It just looks that way."

"Oh shut it," Jade told them both. "We're getting out of here." She was already running.

Rich hurried to catch up. "How?"

"Tractor!" she yelled back at him.

It would be close, she could tell. But they could make it to the tractor before the car reached them. The car was moving slowly, cautiously, skidding across the muddy field. The driver must be afraid he'd lose control. And he could see Jade, Rich and McCain running towards him. He must think they were coming to surrender.

"Hope the keys are in it," said Rich. He was gasping for breath as they ran.

"You should get some exercise," Jade told him.

"What do you think I'm doing?"

The tractor was a dark silhouette against the lights from the approaching car. Jade leaped up on to it, Rich close behind. McCain was round the driver's side. He heaved himself up into the cab. It was tight, but they all just managed to squeeze in. Jade and Rich had to stand, squashed behind the driver's seat.

"The keys there?" asked Jade.

"Who needs keys?" McCain was fumbling under the steering wheel, ripping out wires and twisting them back together. The engine spluttered into life.

The lights were bright – dazzling Jade when she looked back at the car. She could just see the dark shape of someone leaning out of the passenger window.

"Down!" she yelled.

Bullets smashed through the glass of the cab, as the tractor started to move. The car hurtled towards it now as the driver accelerated. The lights disappeared, below the level of the tractor cab and too close for Jade to see.

But she felt the impact as the car smashed into the back of the tractor.

"That won't do them any good," said McCain grimly.

The tractor was moving faster now, its massive tyres gripping easily in the muddy ground while the car slewed off to one side. It had lost a headlight and the bonnet was crumpled.

More gunfire. But it went wide. The car was out of control, sliding across the muddy field.

The tractor bumped down the bank to the river, its huge wheels managing what the lorry couldn't. When they passed the shattered remains of the lorry Jade was surprised they'd even got out of the broken cab, let alone without serious injuries. But even as she thought it, she could feel her shoulder throbbing. There was blood on her hands, and she realised she must be bleeding – cut by the glass from the windscreen. Great.

McCain took the tractor slowly through the river.

"It's wide, but is it deep?" he wondered.

"We'll soon find out," said Rich. His voice was muffled and Jade saw he was eating a bread roll.

"Where did you get that?" she demanded.

He pointed back at the crashed lorry.

"It's not yours," she told him.

"Might be. I ordered some." He shrugged. "Anyway, no one else will want it now."

Further discussion was cut off by more gunfire. The water either side of the tractor was chewed up by bullets. Several pinged off the tractor's side.

"Hold on!" McCain shouted.

The roar of the engine deepened. Water washed across the floor of the tractor's cab. Jade didn't like to think what would happen if it reached the engine.

Then they were climbing, up and out of the river and into the field on the other side.

"We made it!" said Rich. "They must be awful shots."

Jade laughed with relief.

"Still got to get out of the field," McCain warned them.

"Who are those people, and why are they after you?" asked Jade.

Ahead of them, the tractor's headlights picked out another gate. McCain stopped the tractor.

"I'll tell you once we know we're in the clear." He nodded at the gate. "Maybe we should open this one."

"I'll get it," said Rich. He pushed open the door, though he could probably have climbed through the empty space where the glass had been.

A minute later they were driving along a country lane with steep hedges either side. The tractor almost filled the whole road.

"We made it," said Rich. "Amazing."

"Well done," Jade told McCain. "Now perhaps you'll tell us what's going on."

"Got some bad guys after me," said McCain.

"We'd never have guessed," said Rich.

"*Really* bad guys. The worst. I was hoping John – your dad – could help me out."

"I'm sure he would," said Jade, "but he's away on… business."

"I can imagine," said McCain, with a tight smile. The smile faded as he glanced over his shoulder, past Jade and Rich standing by the driver's seat. "Sorry – looks like we spoke too soon."

Jade turned to look. A pair of powerful headlights

was scything through the darkness behind them.

"Could just be someone out for a drive," said Rich.

The car clipped a hedge as it took a corner too fast and too wide. A bullet slammed into the back of the tractor.

"Or not," Rich conceded, ducking down with Jade into as much cover as they could find.

"They must have had a second car," said McCain. "And it looks like this one is going to catch us."

3

The car was weaving back and forth across the road as it came up behind them. But the tractor was so wide and the lane so narrow that there was no way past.

"Only a matter of time before they hit a tyre," said Rich. "Or one of us."

"Any suggestions?" asked Jade, her voice cracking. They'd been in trouble before – several times, in fact, since they'd come to live with their dad. But this was every bit as serious as it got.

A bullet ripped into the metal cage surrounding the cab, making them both duck down even further. McCain was hunched over the steering wheel.

Up ahead, at the limit of the headlights, Rich could make out a dark patch in the high hedge. It might be an opening. "Go right!" he yelled, as he saw it was a single-track lane leading off at right angles.

McCain spun the heavy wheel, the tractor squealed as it turned. There was a smell of burning rubber as the tyres bit into the roadway. For a moment it looked like they weren't going to make it. Then the tractor punched through the side of the hedge. Branches and leaves raked through the cab, scratching Rich's face.

In a moment, they were through. The tractor roared as fast as it would go along the even narrower track. There was grass growing in the middle, and the gravel had worn away. The track was cratered with potholes.

In the road behind, the pursuing car screeched, engine protesting as it tried to follow. And failed. There was an ear-splitting crash as it buried itself in the hedge.

But at once it was reversing, lining up and hurtling down the track after them.

"Farm buildings," Jade shouted, pointing off to the left.

The track swung in a shallow curve round towards the farm. But McCain headed straight for the buildings – across a ploughed field. The tractor lurched and bumped. There was no way the car could follow them – it would have to take the long route. McCain killed the headlights.

"No point in telling them exactly where we are."

But even as he finished speaking, there was a flash of lightning, illuminating the scene brightly.

"Even the gods are on their side," Rich complained. "And any second we're going to get soaked."

"Better than getting shot," Jade told him.

The buildings loomed closer, silhouetted against the deep grey sky. There was a farmhouse, several barns, outbuildings and a cattle shed.

"Can we double back?" Jade wondered. "Get back to the road?"

"They might have another car, waiting," said McCain. "And it'll take too long to turn round."

The tractor bumped up on to a paved courtyard outside the farmhouse. Chickens flew up in surprise and fright as the tractor woke them.

"No lights in the house," Rich realised. Now they were closer he could see it was in the process of being rebuilt. "Nobody home."

"Probably no phone either," Jade complained. "Can you get a signal?"

Rich had been trying. He'd called Ardman, their

dad's boss, but the phone wasn't connecting. Maybe it was being jammed somehow, but most likely it was just rubbish coverage in the countryside. He checked again. "Nothing. You getting anything?"

"Who knows," Jade told him. "My phone's charging up back at the cottage."

Rich didn't like to think about when he'd last charged his phone.

The lights from the car seemed a long way back. They'd gained some time, but the car would soon catch them up. Rain was falling heavily now – large drops angled in and quickly drenched Rich.

"Right," McCain announced. "Time to lose ourselves." He turned the tractor towards the group of outbuildings.

The nearest building was a Dutch barn – barely more than a roof supported by metal pillars. Hay and bags of fertilizer were stacked inside, but there was room for the tractor between them. Once through the barn, Rich could see the lights from the car crossing the courtyard behind them, picking out the bales of hay.

McCain turned the tractor towards another barn. This one was a proper building, the doors standing open.

"What if there's no way out?" said Jade.

"Let's hope there is."

"Good plan," she muttered.

The barn was full of farm machinery. The tractor scraped past ploughs and seed drills; a combine harvester. There were doors at the back – mercifully standing open like those at the front.

"Don't think much of the farmer's security," McCain shouted above the sound of the tractor echoing round the barn.

"He's in the middle of nowhere," Rich pointed out.

Outside the barn, a grassy bank led down steeply into a large field. The edges were lost in darkness. Water was already running off the paved area and down the slope as the rain got even heavier. As soon as they were out of the back of the barn, McCain turned the tractor so it was hidden behind the building. The car's lights spilled out of the barn as it approached.

"Out – quick!" McCain ordered. He had to shout over the sound of the engine, the thunder, and the pounding of the rain.

As soon as they were out of the tractor, McCain spun the wheel, pointing the tractor down the slope into the field. Guessing what he was doing, Rich grabbed a brick from a pile holding the barn doors open.

"This any good?"

McCain smiled a thank you, and took the brick. He braced himself against the door of the cab as he wedged the brick down on the accelerator. The tractor started to move off, gathering speed, and McCain jumped clear. He rolled like a paratrooper, coming up quickly and running with Rich and Jade for the next building.

Seconds later, the car emerged from the barn behind them, speeding after the tractor as it careered down the hill into the field, skidding and slewing in the mud.

"They'll soon find it's empty," said Jade.

"But they won't know where we jumped ship, or even if we all got out at the same time," McCain pointed out. "With luck they'll assume we bailed out in the field somewhere and legged it. The rain will make it hard for them to find any tracks or see very far."

"But they'll come looking," said Rich. "We need a really good hiding place, and we need it fast."

The farmhouse would have been the most

comfortable, but also the most obvious hiding place. Rich was getting tired and he was willing to risk it – their pursuers would probably assume they had jumped off the tractor in the field and escaped into the darkness. But McCain was more cautious. "Not the house. Unless you want to wake up with someone's gun to your head."

There was a small hayloft above the barn. Rich was lucky to find the ladder up to it in the dark. The only light was from his mobile phone, and the battery wouldn't last much longer. He needed to preserve it till he could get a signal and call for help. They climbed up the rickety wooden ladder, pulling it up behind them.

It didn't seem that the hayloft was used any more. But there was enough straw and old sacking to gather together into three makeshift mattresses. They positioned themselves so they had a good view down over the farm machinery below. The rain was hammering on the bare tiles just above them. Water trickled in where the roof needed mending.

"What if they come back?" said Jade.

"Stay hidden," said McCain. "There's no way they can know where we are. When it's light, and we can see what we're doing, we'll make a break for it. Maybe flag down a car in the lane outside. But I don't fancy trying to find civilisation in this." His words were punctuated by another flash of lightning.

"The farmhouse is being renovated," said Rich. "There must be builders, workmen, someone to look after those chickens if nothing else."

"And if they come back and do find us?" Jade insisted.

Rich pointed to the combine harvester below. "We'll use that. It's a step up from a tractor, and we can give them a damned good threshing!"

Jade stifled a smile. "Let's hope they don't come back then, if bad jokes are all we've got going for us."

"We should get some sleep," said McCain. "I've a feeling it's going to be a busy and tiring day tomorrow."

Despite the situation, Rich managed to doze. He woke with straw poking painfully into his ear, and the first light of day creeping through the holes in the roof where the water had come through during the night. The rain had stopped and the morning was bright and clear.

Rich's phone still had no signal, but there was enough light to get a decent picture with the camera.

So he pulled out the photograph of Dad, Dex Halford, Ferdy McCain and the other soldier, and smoothed it out. The rain hadn't been kind to it, and the edges were ragged. But he managed to get a decent photo of the snapshot on his phone camera.

Then he wrote a quick text message to Dex Halford and sent it together with the photo: "jade & me with mccain big trouble help!" Of course, it didn't get sent as there was no signal. But as soon as there was, he knew it would go. Not that it would do much good if he couldn't talk to Halford, but with luck Halford would call him back and the call would get through. Although Rich had no idea where they were, so asking for help might not be so useful...

McCain was already awake, sitting behind a bale of hay looking out down into the barn. As Rich joined him, he put his finger to his lips and pointed down into the barn. Rich could see the silhouette of a man against the open doors, the low morning sunlight streaming past him.

"Farmer?" Rich whispered.

McCain shook his head. The figure moved slightly, looking round the barn, and Rich could see now that he was holding a handgun.

"Perhaps he's out shooting rabbits," Jade's voice whispered in Rich's ear. She took shelter behind the hay bale with Rich and McCain, and together they watched the man making his way slowly through the maze of farm machinery.

He moved with practised ease, gun at the ready. His movements were slow and measured, with sudden bursts of speed as he checked each and every possible hiding place methodically and with professional care.

At one point, as he stepped back from inspecting the combine harvester, the man glanced up. Rich was pretty sure they were hidden in the shadows, but even so he drew back. Beside him Jade mirrored his movement. But McCain stayed exactly where he was, as if daring the man to see him.

The man was wearing an expensive-looking dark suit with a white shirt and modest tie. His hair was black, slicked back and oiled. His face was pale brown, and weathered like old stone. One of his eyebrows ended abruptly above the eye, continuing as a pale scar that curled down his left cheek.

For several moments he stared up at the hay loft. Rich was sure he could see McCain, but abruptly the man turned away and continued his search of the barn below.

After what seemed an age, the man left the barn. Rich could hear voices outside, then the distant sound of a car.

"Think we're OK?" asked Jade.

"Think we had a lucky escape," Rich told her. "But we should get out of here."

"Agreed," said McCain. "And despite what Rich thinks, I don't fancy making a break for it on a combine harvester, so let's see what the alternatives are."

There was a garage behind the farmhouse. Rich thought it would probably be filled with more farm machinery, but instead there as a dirty green Range Rover. They all climbed inside. Rich and Jade got in the back, leaving McCain alone in the front.

"You still haven't told us who these people are and what they want," said Jade to McCain as he got the engine started. She was leaning forward, over the back of the passenger seat.

"Not much to tell," he admitted. "They're not nice people, as you've probably gathered. And they want money. Simple as that."

"What did you do to upset them?" Rich wondered.

"They paid me to do a job. I was unable to complete it, through no fault of my own. They want their money back."

He put the Range Rover into gear and reversed it out of the garage on to the courtyard.

"Maybe you should just pay them their money," said Jade as they started down the track to the lane.

"Maybe I should. But I've spent it. They're not very happy about that."

"We could tell," said Rich. "So why come to Dad?"

"He's a useful guy when you're in a tight spot. And he has connections that might help. I was hoping he could bargain for me, get me more time."

"Ardman might help," said Rich.

"Dad's boss," said Jade quickly, glaring at Rich. "He has connections too."

They turned out on to the lane, heading the same way as they had the night before.

"Best not go back to your cottage. They might be watching it."

"I'll call Ardman," said Rich. "As soon as I can get a signal. Hey – have you got a mobile?" If McCain's was with a different operator he might have a signal.

But McCain shook his head. "I left home in a bit of a hurry. Didn't have time to pick it up."

"Tell me about it," said Jade.

Rich checked his mobile again. His text message was no longer in the outbox, so he hoped that meant it had been sent. But he didn't say anything. Best not to raise their hopes until he was sure there was a good reason.

They drove for over half an hour before they saw another vehicle. It was still very early in the morning and the country lanes were empty. A silver Mercedes pulled out of a side road behind them. It kept its distance. The car was still with them as they reached the outskirts of a village.

"We should stop and borrow a phone or something," said Jade.

McCain checked the rear-view mirror. "I'd rather keep going," he said. "I think that car's following us."

Rich twisted round to see. The car was still keeping its distance. "How can you tell?"

"Let's find out."

McCain slowed as they entered a 30mph limit. Another sign said: *Welcome to Boscombe.* The Mercedes drew closer. Rich could see the driver clearly now, but he looked very ordinary. Just a man on his way to work.

"I think I recognise the driver," McCain confirmed. "His colleagues call him 'Nail', because he's such a hardcase."

He put his foot down, and sure enough, the car behind began to speed up too. At the same moment, Rich's phone rang.

It was voicemail. He struggled to hear the message as the Range Rover tore through the village. A second car had pulled out behind the Mercedes. Its lights were flashing, and after a moment the Merc pulled over to let the car past. It was a dark BMW. The driver was wearing sunglasses, and so was the passenger.

The voice in Rich's ear was hard to hear. Jade was hissing at him, asking who it was.

"Voicemail. From Dex Halford," Rich told her. "He must have got my text."

"You sent him a text?"

"Don't call him back," said McCain. "They may be homing in on your phone. Maybe that's how they found us."

"Can they do that?" asked Jade.

"Oy!" Rich shouted. He'd listened to the whole

message and heard almost none of it. He played it through again. The signal was bad, it kept breaking up. His battery bleeped a warning.

"It's Dex, I got your text, but… except to voicemail. So I hope you get this. McCain's a good guy; you'll be OK with him. Different story… Darrow, but never mind that. I'll get on to Ardman, send... Leave your phone on and we can… Got to go – that's my other phone ringing. Good luck!"

"He's getting on to Ardman to send help," Rich told them.

"How will Ardman find us?" asked Jade.

The BMW roared up close, and McCain weaved the Range Rover across the narrow village street. He took a corner too fast, clipping a parked car. The BMW slowed, allowing them to draw clear again.

"He said to leave my phone on. I guess they can trace it too," said Rich.

They were leaving the village. There were two dark BMWs behind them now, but no sign of the Mercedes.

"Can we keep ahead of them, at least till help arrives?" Jade asked.

"How long will that be?" asked McCain. "We don't have a lot of fuel."

"And my phone doesn't have a lot of…" Rich's phone beeped again. The display faded and died.

"Oh great," said Jade. "Now they'll never find us."

"So we have to get away from these jokers on our own," said McCain. "Let's see if we can shake them off."

The road ahead turned in a tight bend. McCain dropped down a gear and took the bend fast. Then he stamped hard on the brake.

Hovering above the road in front of them, just a few feet off the ground and almost blocking the width of the lane, was a black helicopter. The side door was open, and a woman dressed in a dark trouser suit and wearing sunglasses leaned out. Her long, dark hair was blowing round her face, but she was utterly focused on what she was doing.

She was holding a rifle, and she was aiming it at the Range Rover skidding towards her, smoke rising from the protesting tyres.

4

Just as it seemed the Range Rover was screeching to a halt, McCain took his foot off the brake and floored the accelerator. The tyres spun on the roadway before starting to grip and the vehicle shot forwards – straight at the helicopter.

The woman with the rifle fired. Jade saw the flash from the muzzle. From the angle it looked like she'd been aiming for the tyres, hoping to disable the Range Rover so the men in the cars behind could catch them.

But the Range Rover's change of speed had thrown out her aim and the bullet thumped harmlessly into the asphalt. The woman had no time for a second shot. The helicopter was so low over the road that the Range Rover was heading straight for it...

The pilot reacted quickly. The nose of the helicopter moved upwards. Grit and dirt was blown across the road by the updraft as the helicopter started to rise.

"Hold on!" shouted McCain, as the Range Rover continue to accelerate.

"We're going to hit!" yelled Rich.

The windscreen exploded as the Range Rover slammed into one of the helicopter's skids. McCain pushed the crazed glass out of the way and kept going. The Range Rover zig-zagged down the narrow lane, grazing a hedge and bumping over the verge before McCain got it under control again.

Jade turned to look out the back window. The helicopter was still trying to climb. But it was twisting awkwardly in the air, thrown off balance by the impact. It tilted too far to one side and the end of a rotor blade touched the surface of the road.

With a wrenching of metal, the blade was torn off and went spinning away. The helicopter fell like a stone, blocking the road. The woman in the dark suit and sunglasses struggled out of the side door, which was now at the top of the helicopter.

There was a distant squeal of brakes. Jade saw the

woman knocked clear as the helicopter jolted with the impact of the BMW.

"Way to go!" yelled Rich as they took the next bend and the wreckage of the helicopter disappeared from sight.

"But where do we go?" asked Jade. "What if they've got another helicopter? These people are *serious*."

"They certainly are," said McCain. "I'm open to suggestions. We need somewhere we can lose ourselves, maybe in a crowd. Lots of people, and places we can't be spotted from the air. Somewhere we can ditch this vehicle without it being too conspicuous."

"With a broken windscreen?" said Rich. "Some hope."

"Hey," Jade realised. "We just came through Boscombe, didn't we?"

There was a brown tourist attraction road sign coming up at the junction ahead of them. Jade had already guessed what it said. McCain slowed as they approached the turn.

Rich laughed. "I've always wanted to go there."

"Ideal," McCain agreed.

The Range Rover turned into the road leading towards *Boscombe Heights Adventure Park*.

They had to wait in the car park for half an hour for the adventure park to open. But it gave them time to make use of the toilets in the car park – not least to have a quick wash and get some of the mud off their clothes and hands and faces. By the time they'd cleaned themselves up to look reasonably respectable, there was already a queue. But as it was a school day they didn't have to wait long before McCain was paying for tickets and they were through the turnstiles and into *Boscombe Heights*.

"We should be at school," said Rich, watching a group of children being lectured by their teacher about appropriate behaviour.

"Tell me about it," said Jade. "Miss Fredericks will have a fit."

Rich grinned. "She'll probably try to call Dad. Good luck to her."

"We'll need a note," said Jade. "Dear Miss Fredericks, sorry Rich and Jade weren't in school, but they were being chased by gunmen and had to escape on a tractor before having to drive into a pursuing helicopter and seek refuge in an adventure park."

"And she'll say, "That's all right this once. But make sure it doesn't happen again.""

They both laughed. Jade was feeling the tension ease as they walked through the park. There was a semblance of normality as they joined a queue of people waiting to take a turn at a stall where you had to fish plastic ducks out of a pond with a fishing rod and line.

"I'd rather try out *Lightning Strike*," said Rich. He pointed to a growing queue nearby. People were waiting to get into a tunnel leading into a huge mountain. Above the mountain the metal track of rollercoaster ride rose and dipped alarmingly.

"Looks dangerous," said Jade. "Why do people do that?"

"It looks great. Why do we have to go on this duck thing?" Rich asked.

"Because it's free with the ticket," McCain told him. "Like the main rides, you get one go each on Hook-a-Duck. And it gives me a chance to check we're not being followed."

"We should find a phone," said Rich. "Call Halford again and tell him where we are."

"Once we're sure it's safe," said McCain. He turned away, scanning the people arriving through the turnstile gates behind them.

"Don't know about you," said Jade quietly to Rich, "but I usually want to call for help when it *isn't* safe."

"He knows what he's doing," said Rich. "I guess. Dex Halford seems to think he's OK, so we should stick with him and do what he says."

"I suppose," Jade agreed, but she wasn't convinced.

A broad-shouldered man nudged Rich on the shoulder, startling him. Jade almost laughed at her brother's expression. Then the man handed him a fishing rod.

"Your turn, sonny," he said.

McCain was still watching the people coming through the gates when they'd hooked their ducks. If your duck had a cross painted underneath, you won a prize.

"I won a beetle," Rich announced proudly.

"I didn't," said Jade.

"Here, look." Rich's beetle was only a couple of inches long and made of thin metal. It was just a painted hollow shape, but there was another strip of metal welded underneath it. Rich pushed the strip of metal with his thumb and it clicked in and then sprang out again with a distinctive 'click-clack' noise. He did it again.

"OK, we get the idea," Jade told him as he kept doing it. "Well done – you fished a plastic duck out of a paddling pool."

"It takes skill," Rich told her. "You're just jealous."

"Course I am. I've always wanted a toy beetle." Jade smiled. "Used to want to swap my brother for one."

"Hey!"

"Children," McCain chided. "Come on, let's get further from the gates, I'm not convinced we lost our friends back there."

"Neither am I," said Rich. He pointed at the turnstiles, where two men in dark suits wearing sunglasses were pushing through a group of children on a school trip.

"That way too," Jade realised. There were two more suited men in sunglasses approaching along a narrow path from the direction of one of the big rides.

"Time we were going," said McCain.

He pushed into the deepest part of the queue for *Lightning Strike*, Rich and Jade following close behind.

"Stick together," McCain called over his shoulder. "But if we get separated we meet back at Hook-a-Duck in one hour, right?"

"Right," Jade called back.

Rich didn't answer. And when Jade turned to look for him, she found he was nowhere in sight. "Typical," she muttered.

Before she could waste any more time looking, McCain grabbed her wrist and pulled her after him. "He'll find us," he said.

"He'd better."

A familiar-looking dark-haired woman in a plain trouser suit and wearing sunglasses was standing to the side of the queue. For a moment, her shaded eyes seemed to fix on Jade.

Rich was right behind Jade and McCain. Then a fat man pushed in front of him, dragging a chubby boy holding an ice cream. The end of the ice cream broke free and fell. Rich jumped back in time to avoid getting it down his shirt.

When the boy and the man moved away, Jade was gone.

He looked round desperately. She couldn't be far away. He thought he caught a glimpse of Jade's distinctive blonde hair. But it was immediately lost in the crowd of people pushing towards *Lightning Strike* ride as the queue moved forwards. Rich felt himself being pulled along with the crowd.

He was about to step out of the line and head in the direction he thought Jade and McCain must have gone, when he saw the woman. Rich recognised her at once from the helicopter, and he quickly turned away.

She was heading straight for him. Rich braced himself, ready to run, but the woman pushed through the queue a few metres in front of Rich and kept going. Somehow she'd missed him, distracted by something else. Rich saw her disappear into a group of school children, forcing her way through.

The queue moved again. If Rich didn't leave now, he'd be inside the tunnel. He couldn't leave then without making a fuss and drawing attention to himself. He looked round once more to be sure he was safe. And found he wasn't.

There was a man in dark glasses standing within a few metres of him. The man was looking the other way, and Rich could see the coil of wire leading to his concealed earpiece. *These people have some serious technology and resources*, Rich thought. Who exactly were they? The queue edged forwards again. It was now or never.

The man turned, and Rich ducked down,

pretending to tie his shoelace. He was forced to stand up again as the people behind pushed forwards. Rich was inside the tunnel now, edging closer to *Lightning Strike*. Ahead of him the queue arrived at a small platform where the set of linked carriages that carried you through the ride drew up. People got off on the other side before the people at the front of the queue took their place.

Maybe Rich could spot Jade from above, he thought. But he knew that wouldn't be much help. Unless he could make her see him – which would draw attention to himself, he was sure – she'd be sure to have moved on by the time the ride ended. But Rich realised he could just climb across the carriage when his turn came, instead of taking the ride, and leave by the exit on the other side.

It didn't work out quite like that.

Rich reached the front of the queue and prepared to shuffle quickly across the bench seat of one of the front sections and get off the other side. He glanced round before he got off – and saw the man with dark glasses in the queue behind him. The good news was that he hadn't spotted Rich. The bad news was that from where the man was standing, if Rich stood up or climbed out now that everyone else had cleared the exit platform, the man couldn't fail to spot him.

He'd have to go on the ride after all. A teenage girl climbed in beside Rich and sat down closer to him than she needed. He shuffled away slightly, and earned a coy smile.

The locking bar came down over their knees, holding them in place. Rich glanced quickly over his shoulder. The man in dark glasses had gone. He breathed a sigh of relief. The guy must have decided he'd lost Rich and pushed his way back down the tunnel and out again. By the time the ride was over, he should be long gone.

The girl beside him offered Rich a peppermint. It was green. He was so relieved he took it.

"Thanks."

"'s all right. You get scared?"

"Er, no," said Rich.

"I do. I might scream and grab hold of you." She grinned again, showing off the braces on her teeth. "Just so you know."

Rich nodded dumbly. Maybe he should have taken his chances with the mafia hitman, or whatever he was. Instinctively, Rich turned away, looking round.

The line of linked carriages jerked into motion, and started to move along the track. The locking bar was holding Rich firmly and safely in position.

And three carriages behind him, Rich could see the man in the sunglasses.

The carriages were climbing now, ratcheting up a sharp incline as the rollercoaster was hauled to the top of the first peak. The man in sunglasses was looking over the side, staring down into the crowds below – looking for Rich, Jade and McCain, probably. He had his finger to his ear, and was muttering into his lapel – in touch with others on the ground.

Rich turned quickly away. He had to keep his head down until the end of the ride. With luck he could take his time getting out of the carriage and let the man leave first, without seeing him.

The rollercoaster reached the top of the track. The rails seemed impossibly slender, the slope down incredibly steep. The carriage began to tip forwards. Rich felt his stomach lurch and the rush of adrenaline as the rollercoaster fell. He could almost feel the weight of the carriages behind, pushing him ever faster down the steep slope.

Then they were rushing up the other side. The girl

beside Rich was yelling and grabbing his arm. He turned to look at her. And out of the corner of his eye, he saw that the man in the sunglasses was staring straight ahead – right at him.

Still Rich wasn't too worried. When the previous passengers had got off, he'd seen that the locking bars released in sequence to make sure people left in an orderly manner. The front row released first, then the others in sequence. He'd be out of his seat before the hitman. And he'd be running as soon as he could. Assuming he could shake off the teenage girl now clinging to him. He glanced at her, and decided he could.

How long was the ride? They were rising up another sharp incline. He had to be ready to go. Mustn't get dizzy from the height or the twists. Mustn't let the hitman know he'd been spotted. How much time would he have?

The rollercoaster screamed down again as Rich tried to remember how long a delay there had been between the locking bars lifting. The ride twisted suddenly sideways along a banked curve. The sound of the wheels rumbling on the track was like thunder.

Rich glanced back as the carriages slowed again,

rising up for the next drop. It was a long slow incline, the carriages locking into a chain that hauled them slowly upwards, drawing out the tension as the rollercoaster rose higher and higher. The people in the park below were little more than dots.

But Rich wasn't looking at them. He was staring in horror at the hitman three carriages behind. He was watching the man haul himself out from under the locking bar and climb into the carriage in front. He was coming for Rich.

5

People yelled and shouted. The man stepped into the next carriage, his foot between the two people sitting there, as he took another huge step over the back of the next seat.

The rollercoaster inched its way up the slope. Would the man get to Rich before it reached the top and headed down the slope again?

A woman with a small boy grabbed at the man as he stepped past them. She was shouting at him, her face red with anger and fear as he jostled past. The man ignored them and kept going. He reached the front of the carriage. There was a gap between it and the next one, but the man just jumped. He landed on the back of the carriage in front, and hauled himself onwards.

He was getting into a rhythm now. The metronomic clack of the chain was slowing by comparison to the man's movements. He'd reach Rich well before the rollercoaster arrived at the top of the slope.

Rich looked down. It must be over twenty metres to the ground. The ride was built out of linked and braced struts of steel, but they were too far apart for him to have any hope of climbing down the side.

There was only one carriage ahead of Rich. He could see an empty seat right at the back of it. A woman had put her bag beside her to stop anyone else getting in.

The girl clung tightly to Rich's arm. "This is going to be *soooo* scary," she wailed happily.

"You're telling me," said Rich, pulling his arm free.

The girl watched him in open-mouthed astonishment as he heaved the locking bar up an inch, and prised his legs out from underneath.

"It was fun," Rich told her, "but not really scary enough for me. See you." And he climbed over into the seat in front.

The look on the girl's face was mirrored on those of the two young men in the seat in front.

"Coming through!" Rich yelled. There was just

room for his foot between them. He balanced on the bench seat before taking a giant stride over to the next one.

The carriage jumped slightly as it went over a join in the rails. For a moment Rich wobbled, unbalanced. He grabbed for one of the men's shoulders, but missed. His arms windmilled and he felt himself falling to one side.

A hand grabbed him. It was the girl he'd been sitting next to. She caught his arm from behind and held on tight until he was steady again.

"Thanks," said Rich.

Further down the rollercoaster there were people shouting and pointing. The hitman was only a few seats back now.

"If you don't like me," the girl told him, "just say so."

"You're great," Rich assured her. "But I have to go. Sorry." He added another "sorry" to the two men, and took the next step, into the front of the carriage. A mother and small boy stared at him in undisguised amazement as he stepped between them. Rich forced a smile.

They were almost at the top of the incline now. The

hitman stepped on to Rich's old seat. He was shouting something, but Rich couldn't hear him above the yelling of everyone else, the thunder of the wheels on the rails, the wind buffeting him as they rose ever higher.

He had to jump to get to the front carriage. He braced himself. What if the man shot him as he leaped – would it look like an accident? Like he cared, he thought. And jumped.

The back of the carriage rushed up to meet him. But Rich could see he wasn't going to make it. The rollercoaster was moving away as it tipped, as it gathered speed to head down the slope. For a split-second Rich could see down the rails to the bottom. He could see just how far he was going to fall.

Then the whole rollercoaster stopped. It teetered on the brink, just about to fall – a final planned moment of terror for the occupants as they stared down at the abyss. A final planned moment that saved Rich's life as he scrabbled at the back of the carriage and managed to grab hold.

He tumbled over the back and into the empty seat. There was no time to wriggle under the locking bar, so he grabbed hold of it and braced himself. His foot connected with something on the seat. The woman stared at him in horror as her bag went flying over the side. Then the whole rollercoaster was falling.

A sudden flash of light blinded him for a second. He thought for a moment he'd been shot, but there was no blood, no pain.

Rich was sprawled awkwardly across the seat, holding tight to the locking bar as the rollercoaster hurtled down the slope. He felt like his stomach was still somewhere at the top of the ride; he could hear the blood throbbing in his ears.

Then the rollercoaster was levelling out, slowing down. Rich twisted until he was more comfortable, but he couldn't afford to stay where he was. The hitman would be climbing after him any second. The woman beside him was yelling about her bag and hitting Rich. He wanted to tell her it was just a bag, and there were people trying to *kill* him so why was she so annoyed? But the descent had knocked the wind from him and he was still gasping to get it back.

The carriage was almost still now. They were back at the station where they'd got on. The rollercoaster slowed as it reached the platform and somehow Rich managed to roll sideways. His feet met the wooden platform while the carriage was still moving and he almost fell as he staggered clear.

"Hey!" the attendant yelled.

But Rich didn't wait to get told off. He lurched away from the rollercoaster, giddily heading for the exit. How long did he have? How soon before the hitman was after him? Would the girl he'd been sitting next to try to slow the man down or get help?

He didn't have time to find out. The exit tunnel loomed ahead and Rich charged towards it.

Only when he was inside the tunnel did he realise there was someone with him, keeping pace as they ran.

The man was grinning. He popped a green peppermint into his mouth as they ran. Then he grabbed Rich's arm and pushed him hard against the tunnel wall.

"I just want to talk to you, Rich," he said in an American accent.

"Yeah right," said Rich.

The hitman's sunglasses reflected Rich's pale face back at him.

They couldn't go back, Jade knew that. Rich would have to fend for himself. For now the important thing was to get away from the people in dark suits and even darker glasses who were after them. Jade would worry about finding Rich again later, once they were safe.

She stuck close to Ferdy McCain as he pushed through the crowds round the rides. But whatever way she looked, Jade could see one of the men searching for them. She watched in horror as a broad shouldered man in a dark suit suddenly lunged into the crowd just yards away. He hauled out a girl with shoulder-length blonde hair cut a bit like Jade's.

The similarity was superficial, and the man let her go at once. He muttered an apology and moved on, but it scared Jade. "We have to get out of sight, out of the open," she told McCain.

They were in the middle of a group moving slowly towards an old house. The queue looped up a narrow, cobbled driveway to a crooked front door. The door opened and the queue moved forwards. They passed a sign that said: *Professor Horror's House of Terror.*

"As good a place to hide as any," said McCain. The queue stopped and the door closed again.

"If we ever get there," said Jade.

They were near the front now. "We should get inside with the next group," McCain pointed out.

Jade looked round, but they seemed to have got away from their pursuers for the moment. She could see the woman from the helicopter pushing through the back of the queue and hurrying away.

After what seemed an age, the door opened again and an overly cheerful young man ushered in the next group of people.

"Don't get scared in there now," he told Jade as she went in.

Jade glared at him. "Takes more than a visit to Scooby-Doo's house to scare me."

The young man grinned. "Really?"

But Jade wasn't listening. The woman with long dark hair was back. She was standing at the far end of the queue, and she was looking up at Jade. Her eyes were hidden behind her shades, but Jade was sure the woman had seen her. Jade turned and hurried through the door.

A few more people followed, then the door closed. Jade let out a long breath. Maybe the woman hadn't seen her after all.

"You OK?" McCain asked.

"Oh yeah. I just love haunted houses and ghost trains and stuff like that."

They were in a wood-panelled room. Portraits of sinister-looking people were painted directly on to the walls, frames and all. The eyes rolled ridiculously as the portraits watched the people in the room. A small boy laughed and pointed. A girl tried to hide behind her mother.

Electric lights designed to look like candles flickered unconvincingly. A large chandelier hung from the ceiling on a chain, swinging dangerously – it seemed – to and fro.

"At least we're safe in here," said Jade.

But as soon as she said it, the door was flung open again. The woman following them stood silhouetted in the doorway. The young man tried to close the door on her, but she pushed him roughly aside.

Jade looked around frantically for another way out. There wasn't one.

The woman pushed into the room. She reached up and took off her sunglasses. The eyes beneath were almost as dark and sinister, and at once she caught sight of Jade and McCain. Her lips twisted into a smile and she moved through the crowd towards them.

McCain grabbed Jade's hand, dragging her away. Soon they were facing a fireplace painted on to the wall like the portraits. McCain hammered at the wooden panelling, but there was no way out.

They spun round, just as the woman pushed past the last people and stood in front of them. There was no escape now.

6

Jade and McCain had their backs to the fake fireplace. The woman reached inside her jacket, and Jade could guess what she kept there. Would she just shoot them where they stood – in front of so many witnesses?

Suddenly the floor of the room tilted, as if the whole house had been tipped up. The woman staggered back, just as surprised as everyone else. McCain and Jade grabbed for the ridges of the wooden panelling, desperate to avoid being flung after the woman. But they were still easy targets.

Then the lights went out. In the complete and utter darkness people screamed with a mix of terror and delight.

The panel that Jade was holding began to move; it

was sliding away from her. Light spilled into the room from behind the panel. It was a door, and beyond it was a corridor, the floor at an angle and lights flickering on the skewed walls.

"Go!" McCain yelled in Jade's ear.

She didn't need telling twice. Jade ran. She hoped McCain was close behind – and that the woman in the suit, the woman with the gun, was a long way back.

Most people were walking slowly, looking at the pictures on the walls of the passage. Some were optical illusions; some were of fainting Victorian ladies menaced by ghosts and demons. One transformed from a handsome man into a rotting skull as Jade ran past.

"Kids' stuff," she muttered, and kept running.

Straight into a mass of cobwebs strung across the passage. To her horror and embarrassment, Jade shrieked. She clawed at the strands clinging to her face, and kept running. There was a loud bang behind her. Was it part of the haunted house stuff, a door banging or a gunshot?

The passageway turned so abruptly that Jade almost ran into the wall. A continuation of the passage was painted on it – another illusion. But to the side, the passage opened out into a large ballroom.

A glass screen separated off the side of the room, so that Jade was in effect still in a corridor. Through the glass she could see the rest of the ballroom. An enormous chandelier hung from the ceiling. Classical statues stood in alcoves. Huge windows were covered with lavish velvet curtains. And through the room, dancers moved elegantly and effortlessly to the slightly tinny sound of Sait-Saens' distinctive *Danse Macabre*.

Yet, as they danced, Jade realised they were not real. They were becoming insubstantial, like ghosts, and Jade could see through them. The dancers then reappeared as if solid, only now their clothes were faded and torn, dusty and grey. And the faces of the handsome men and beautiful women were pale, fleshless skulls.

Another illusion, Jade realised, but she didn't have time to admire it. More people were pushing into the ballroom area behind her, marvelling at the dance. They gasped as the dancers changed again. For the moment there seemed to be no way out. A hidden door would open, but only after everyone was in the ballroom and had enjoyed the illusion. Everyone – including the woman with the gun.

She couldn't see McCain. Maybe he'd managed to slip away and get out of this nightmare haunted house, but for Jade it was a trap. There was only one quick way out. The glass partition between the audience and the dance floor came up to Jade's shoulder. She braced her hands on the top of it, then hauled herself up and over.

She tilted and twisted over the top, landing heavily on her back, but she was up at once. She needed to hide somewhere before the woman saw her – assuming she hadn't watched Jade vault over the screen.

It was at this point that Jade realised how the illusion of the dance was achieved. The dancers were on film, projected on to a glass screen behind the partition, reaching up almost to the ceiling. And now Jade was trapped between the partition and that screen, in a narrow glass-walled corridor.

The woman was pushing through the crowd. People were shouting at Jade, telling her not to be so stupid and to stop mucking about.

"There's always one person who has to spoil it all, isn't there," a fat man said.

Jade got some satisfaction from seeing him shoved heavily against the partition as the woman in the trouser suit barged through. But it didn't last. As the woman prepared to vault the partition after Jade, her jacket flapped open, revealing a shoulder holster at her left armpit.

Jade ran. She had no idea if there was a way out, or if she'd be trapped by the wall. But she put her hand against the glass and ran. When her hand disappeared into space just a metre from the ballroom wall, she almost cried out for joy. The screen didn't reach right to the end; there was just room for Jade to squeeze through.

The woman could probably follow, but Jade was slim, and even if she was pretty slim too the woman had a bulky jacket — and a gun. It was a struggle, but Jade got painfully round the end of the screen, and on to the empty dance floor.

Looking back, she could see the dancers reflected on the glass. This time they were dancing the other way. A skull stared out at Jade, and from behind it she saw the woman's determined face as she watched Jade for a second, before running for the gap at the end of the glass wall.

There was a door at the back of the ballroom. Jade had no idea if it was even a real door, but she wrenched it open, and was relieved to find it gave out into another corridor. From the other side, it looked like a panel in the wall – probably for maintenance access.

She was in another corridor, obviously further round the tour. With luck she was close to the end, but she had no way of knowing. And the woman would be after her soon. Jade set off at a run down the corridor, but she didn't know if she was heading for the exit, or would meet the rest of the tour coming the other way...

The ceiling ahead of her was moving. It was lower than the part of the corridor she was leaving, and curved. In fact, as she approached, Jade could see that the corridor floor became a bridge through a cylinder that was turning slowly. The cylinder's surface was covered with shining stars and planets like the night sky.

There didn't seem to be much point to the turning cylinder, so Jade ran on. And wished she hadn't. There were handrails along the side of the corridor and she grabbed at one of them. Even though Jade knew it was the ceiling and walls that were turning and not the floor, her mind and body were telling her the floor was tilting and she clung desperately to the rail as she tried to keep her balance.

She inched her way along, one foot in front of the other, one step at a time. Jade tried to fix her attention on the dark end of the bridge where it became a corridor again. She told herself the floor was steady, that she wasn't being turned upside down, but everything she saw told her that wasn't true.

Her head was spinning as much as the cylinder and she began to feel dizzy and a bit sick. She wasn't even halfway over yet. The woman couldn't be far behind. Just focus, Jade told herself; just don't look at the walls or the ceiling.

Then she realised. She shouldn't look at anything. The way to get across quickly was simple. She closed her eyes and immediately she felt better – she could tell her feet were steady on a solid floor. Keeping hold of the rail, she hurried across the bridge.

When she felt the end of the rail, Jade opened her eyes again – just in time to avoid walking into the wall at the end of the corridor where it turned sharply.

She looked back at the bridge that had caused her so much trouble. The woman in the suit was running towards her, and had reached the far end of the bridge. Jade hesitated, expecting the woman to stagger and clutch at the handrail, and look as daft and disorientated as she must have done.

But she just kept running, like there was no problem. Like she'd been trained for this sort of thing. Jade didn't hesitate any longer.

The corridor opened out into a platform area, with metal barriers to guide the people into queues beside a set of rails in the floor. The rails arrived from and disappeared into a low tunnel that looked like it was hewn from solid rock. As Jade was debating which way to go down the tunnel, there was a rumble of sound and a small carriage arrived.

It was like a miniature horse-drawn open-topped carriage, only with no horse. A swirl of mist puffed out from under its wheels so that it seemed almost to float along its track. The sides were daubed with swirls of luminous paint. When the carriage stopped beside the platform, Jade climbed in without a second thought.

The carriage didn't move. The sound of the woman's footsteps echoed down the corridor. Her shadow fell distorted across the platform where Jade had been standing. Jade was trapped.

Then the carriage gave an unsteady lurch and started to move off. The woman skidded to a halt on the platform area, and Jade ducked down, but behind her, she could hear the faint rumble of another carriage arriving.

Jade wasn't sure if the woman had seen her, but she had to assume so. There wasn't really anywhere else she could have gone. The carriage was moving steadily, and a locking bar had come down over her legs so it would be hard to get out. Not that there was anywhere to go, as the carriage was running through the rocky tunnel. Jade's best hope was to get to the other end of this ride, then make a run for it before the woman could get out of her own carriage.

She could see the tunnel ending up ahead. A spray of mist drifted down from the roof forming a curtain. It was cold and clammy against Jade's face and she blinked it away.

When she opened her eyes again, she almost screamed. A pirate was coming at her. A black patch covered one of the pirate's eyes, while the other was an empty socket. His clothes were ragged and torn, his bony hands clutching a rusty cutlass that curved through the air towards Jade.

At the last moment it stopped. The pirate figure swayed at the end of its mechanism before being hauled back to lunge again at the next carriage.

"There's a seriously sick mind behind this ride," Jade muttered. Rich would love it, she thought. But it wasn't her sort of thing at all. Past the zombie pirate, Jade could see she was now travelling through a foggy graveyard. Tombstones leaned at drunken angles, chipped and cracked. Two spades were stuck in a mound of earth by a freshly dug grave.

With the fog swirling round the fake grass and polystyrene monuments, this might be her best chance of escape. Jade hauled herself out from under the locking bar, scraping her knees painfully. She glanced back, waiting until the fog seemed even deeper, then jumped from the small carriage.

The ground was hard – wooden. Jade stifled a cry of pain, and kept low so she was wreathed by the smoky mist. She crawled quickly away into the cemetery, and slumped behind the largest tombstone she could find.

The rails curved round, snaking through the graveyard area to get maximum use from it. Jade's empty carriage was soon passing close by, and she realised there wouldn't be much cover when the next carriage passed – the woman would have a clear view of Jade crouching behind the grave stone.

Except that when the carriage did go past a few moments later, it was also empty. The woman had gone.

Jade almost stood up in surprise, but immediately realised that wouldn't be a good idea, and instead pressed herself low to the damp, misty ground. The woman must be out in the graveyard too – looking for Jade. She crawled after the carriages, keeping as low to the ground as she could, and making as little noise as possible. With hindsight, maybe she'd have done better to stay on board – the woman must have seen her getting out and followed. Her best option now was to follow the carriages to the way out of this smoky death-trap.

Suddenly, the ground that Jade was on moved. It was heaving itself upwards – tilting and turning. She gasped out loud in fear and surprise as she was rolled aside. The wooden lid of a coffin sprang up and fell to one side. The pale form of a skeleton sat up. Its head turned and it stared sightlessly at Jade. Then the jaw dropped open and it started to cackle with unearthly laughter.

Jade rolled quickly away, shaking with fear. "Just for kids," she muttered to herself over and over. Another dark tombstone loomed out of the swirling mist. "It's just for kids. It's not real. It's *not* real."

"It may not be real," an American voice said. "But *this* is. And believe me, you're in big trouble."

What Jade had taken for a tombstone was the woman. As Jade looked up, she reached into her jacket. She was taking something out – not the gun, something from her pocket. It looked like a leather wallet.

Jade froze. The woman was staring down at her. There was nowhere to go, nowhere to hide.

Then a spade split through the misty air and slammed into the woman's back. She staggered forwards, her face a mask of surprise and pain. The spade flashed again. It caught her only a glancing blow on the head, but it was enough to send the woman crashing to the floor. McCain chucked the spade down after her, and hauled Jade to her feet.

"Come on," he said. "Let's get out of here."

Together they ran after one of the carriages that was disappearing into the side of a cobwebbed mausoleum.

The rails dipped into a dark tunnel. There was a dim light at the end of it. McCain and Jade ran towards the light. Another of the carriages turned into the tunnel behind them, picking up speed as it started down the slope.

"It's going to catch us!" said Jade.

Ahead of them, the dim light suddenly flared and brightened. Then, just as abruptly it faded again.

Jade was racing down the slope now. She almost twisted her ankle as it caught on one of the rails. She could hear the rumble of the carriage close behind her. McCain was a silhouette sprinting ahead, but any moment, the carriage would roll into both of them.

Then finally, they emerged from the tunnel. McCain leaped to one side, Jade dived to the other, and the carriage shot past them. It started to slow immediately, the rails rising uphill again to take the carriages through the next part of the haunted house tour.

The mad scientist's laboratory.

It looked like the converted dungeons of a medieval castle. The place was lit up brightly by another flash of lightning. A wooden workbench was covered with glassware – test tubes and flasks, bubbling liquids and a brain in a jar. Huge metal coils ran up into a vaulted stone roof. Cables and pipes hung down. A large body lay on an operating table – mercifully covered by an oil-stained sheet.

Thankfully, there was no sign their pursuer.

McCain picked himself up and grinned at Jade as she too got to her feet. But then she saw his grin fade as he stared over her shoulder.

Jade whirled round.

A figure stepped from the shadowy alcove behind her and a tall man dressed in a dark suit reached out for Jade. He was just inches away from her, and there was no way she could escape. His lips parted in a horrible smile.

7

Though he tried not to show it, Rich was impressed. An area of the car park had been cordoned off, and a black helicopter stood in the middle of it. The side door was open and the pilot sat there, his legs dangling over the side. It was a big helicopter – bigger than the one McCain had driven into, and large enough to carry half a dozen people easily.

"Come on, son," said the man in the suit and dark glasses. He nudged Rich forward, though he sounded and seemed deferential.

But then, Rich reminded himself, the man had a gun, so he could afford to be. "My name is Rich," he told the man – it was about as much defiance as he could muster. His heart was still pounding and his legs were still weak from the chase over the rollercoaster.

"Sure thing, Rich," the man drawled in his American accent as they approached the helicopter. "And my name's Chuck."

"Good American name."

A smile appeared beneath the dark glasses. "Short for Charles. That's a good British name."

Several people had gathered round the edge of the taped off area, watching with interest. They probably thought it was some sort of display or exhibit. Rich wondered if he could shout to them for help, tell them that he was being taken away against his will and his sister was in trouble too. But he didn't want to involve anyone else. Who knew how desperate these guys were? They had guns, fast cars, helicopters... They were pretty serious.

Too serious, he suddenly thought, to be chasing someone who just owed them money or a favour. What was really going on?

Then he reached the helicopter. The pilot eased himself back inside, so that another man could lean forward from one of the passenger seats.

"Hello, Rich. It's been a while."

Rich just stared. "You?! What are you doing here?"

The man's teeth were sharp and pointed and stained blood red. His jacket was pinned to him. His face was a pasty mask. He reached out a gloved hand, as if in greeting.

"My name," the man said, his voice accented, scratchy and echoing, "is Count Dracula. Welcome to my domain."

Now that Jade looked properly, she saw that he had not stepped out of the alcove, but slid forward on a little trolley. She could hear the whirr of the mechanism as his head tilted slightly. It was disconcerting the way the voice came not from the mannequin, but from a speaker on the floor close by.

"The children of the night," the spectral voice added, "what music they make..."

Then the figure slid slowly back into the shadows. The laboratory echoed for a moment with his theatrical laughter.

"This place is seriously spooky," said Jade.

"I think that's kind of the idea," McCain told her.

"Yeah, right. Whatever. Let's get out of here before that spooky woman finds us again."

They followed the railway tracks through the

laboratory. Behind them, Jade could hear the Dracula mannequin going through its act again. The tracks led to large wooden double doors that were firmly closed. The carriages seemed to keep going through even between groups of visitors, and as one of the little carriages approached, the doors swung open to let it through. Jade and McCain hurried after the empty carriage before the doors closed again.

They were in another corridor. The walls looked like rough, flaking stone. But when Jade touched them she could feel it was just painted polystyrene. Ahead, she could see another small platform area, like the one where she had originally boarded a carriage. The illuminated sign beyond that was a relief – it said: EXIT.

But before they reached the platform and the exit, there was one more fright.

A skeleton dropped down in front of them. Its jaw dropped open and more laughter echoed round the corridor. Then, just as suddenly, it was gone again.

Jade closed her eyes and breathed deeply.

"You can see why there are warnings to people with weak hearts," said McCain, more amused than surprised.

"To think people pay for this sort of thing," said Jade. She shook her head sadly and hurried towards the exit doors.

The doors opened easily. Outside, a group of people were laughing and joking – their trip round the haunted house just finished. Jade realised she and McCain had almost caught up with the group in front of theirs. But no one spared them more than a glance as they emerged, blinking, into the sunshine.

Jade looked back at the lop-sided house towering above them. "Definitely one for Rich," she murmured. "I wonder where he is now. I hope he's OK."

The man in the helicopter gestured for Rich to get in. He was in his forties, well-built with a rugged face and deep-set eyes. He was someone that Rich and Jade had come to know very well indeed – a friend and former colleague of their father's. He was also one of the men in the photograph that Rich still had in his pocket. It was Dex Halford.

"Forgive me not getting out," said Halford as Rich sat on the uncomfortable seat beside him. Halford slapped his leg, which Rich knew was artificial below the knee. He'd lost his leg in a firefight in Afghanistan, and only escaped with his life because John Chance had carried him for miles.

"What's going on?" demanded Rich. "What are you doing here? Where's Jade?"

"I was hoping *you'd* know that," said Halford. "After I got your call, I rang Ardman. Then I tried to call you back."

"No battery," said Rich. He shook his head, trying to work it all out. He pointed at Chuck who was standing on guard beside the helicopter. "But these guys, they're the ones trying to kill us."

"Actually, they're the ones trying to save you."

"I don't get it."

"They're affiliated with the CIA."

"You called in the *CIA*?"

"Not exactly. They were here already, hot on the heels of a rather unpleasant mercenary they've been trying to track down for a while."

Rich swallowed, he suddenly felt tired and light-headed. "Ferdy McCain?"

"No. Ferdy's no mercenary. He retired from the service and went into business organising adventure holidays. Abseiling, rock climbing, jungle survival, caving. That sort of thing." Halford sighed. "Like I told you, he was a good bloke, Ferdy."

"*Was?* What do you mean – what happened?"

Halford met Rich's puzzled gaze. "When I rang Ardman, to tell him you were on the run with McCain, he was a bit surprised. And worried. It takes a lot to worry Ardman."

Rich nodded. His dad's boss was usually as cool as a cucumber in the arctic. "I know."

"He got in touch with these CIA people, and he told me to find you as soon as possible."

"But why?"

"Because Ferdy McCain was found shot dead at his home in Buckinghamshire yesterday afternoon. That's why."

Rich gaped. "But that's impossible. We've been with him. There must be some mistake."

"No mistake. How do you know the man you are with is actually Ferdy McCain?"

Rich pulled the photograph from his pocket. "He told us. And we recognised him from this."

Halford took the photograph. It was creased and bent, and he smoothed it out on his good knee. "God, those were the days," he said quietly. "Not sure it was fun exactly, but it had its moments.

Iraq…" He shook his head. "What a mess."

"So there has to be a mistake," said Rich, pointing to the figure beside Halford in the photograph. "Because that's definitely the man we were with. OK, it's an old photo, but you can tell it's him."

Halford nodded slowly, his expression grave. "Then we are in serious trouble. Because *this* is Ferdy McCain." He pointed to the other man, the shorter man with a dark moustache beside Rich's dad. "That man," he went on, pointing to the figure that Rich still had his finger over, "is Mark Darrow. One of the nastiest pieces of work I've ever met, and as you know, I've met a few. He's a ruthless mercenary and a hired killer."

Rich could feel the blood draining from his face. "And Jade's with him."

"It's the last place they'll look for us," 'Ferdy McCain' told Jade. "Trust me."

He was busy filling in the adventure park hotel's registration form. "My daughter's birthday," he told the smiling receptionist. "She's fourteen."

Jade turned away. "Do me a favour."

"Kidding," McCain admitted. "Do you have two rooms with a connecting door?"

"Only in the Space Zone," said the receptionist, her smile still fixed perfectly in position. "Is your daughter interested in space?"

"As much of it as I can get," said Jade. "If my brother comes looking for us, let me know at once, will you, please?"

The receptionist frowned. "Your brother?"

"He said he might join us. He wasn't sure," explained McCain. He smiled at the receptionist. "You know what teenagers are like."

"His name is Rich," said Jade. "Short for Richard."

"I'll be certain to let you know," said the receptionist. "Richard Smith. Sure thing. Enjoy your stay."

Halford was getting impatient, and so was Rich.

"Anything from Hunter?" Halford demanded.

"No, sir," replied Chuck, without moving from his position outside the helicopter. "She's not answering. Either she's in a blind spot or her radio's packed up."

"Typical." Halford eased himself past Rich and climbed down on to the tarmac.

Rich followed. There were even more people round the helicopter now. Someone raised a camera and Halford grimaced.

"Ardman will do his nut. So much for low profile."

"Pretend we're part of the show," said Rich.

"Circus, more like."

"Oh, that reminds me," said Chuck. "One of the guys got you a present." He handed Rich a small clear bag. Inside was what looked like a novelty keyring with a large plastic fob attached. Sealed inside the plastic was a picture.

"Souvenir of a great day out," said Chuck.

The picture had been taken on the rollercoaster. Rich remembered the flash of the camera. It showed Rich tumbling over the back of the carriage, legs in the air and a mixture of fear and surprise across his face.

"Thanks," said Rich. "Don't think it's one I'll be showing Dad. Or Jade."

"Here's Hunter, now, sir," said Chuck, moving quickly to the cordon round the helicopter. He lifted the tape for a woman to duck underneath.

Rich recognised her as the woman who had shot at their car tyres from the other helicopter. Just trying to stop them, Halford had told him. He didn't know who the people who'd originally been chasing McCain – or rather Darrow – were. The CIA unit had picked them up that morning from the air and the other cars after them.

"Did you find her?" Halford asked the woman.

She shook her head, and Rich saw an angry bruise developing on the side of her head as her hair moved.

"Sorry, sir." She was American too. "I lost her in the haunted house. Darrow got the drop on me."

"You saw Jade?" said Rich. "Is she all right?"

"So far," the woman – Hunter – said. "I was trying to warn her, show her my ID. I told her she was in trouble, then Darrow jumped me. My radio got smashed when I fell against a gravestone." She held her hand up and sighed. "Don't ask."

"So we have no idea where Jade is," said Rich. "And no way of contacting her."

The woman met Rich's gaze. "Sorry. Maybe she understood my warning."

"What about Darrow?" asked Chuck. His voice was tense and abrupt. "You know our orders, Kate."

"Too many people. I couldn't get a clear shot without the risk of hitting someone else. Maybe even the girl."

"A clear shot?" Rich was appalled. "Who *are* you people? What's this Darrow done that you have orders to shoot him?"

Kate Hunter turned back to Rich. "Believe me, you don't want to know what he's done."

"And now he's escaped," said Halford. "And he's got Jade with him. I'm sorry, Rich, but whether she knows it or not, Jade is a hostage."

8

The control panel in the middle of the room was finished in brushed aluminium, and covered with levers and dials and gauges. Jade pushed a button and a light came on above one of the read-outs. LED numbers flashed up a countdown.

"Sad," she said, shaking her head.

The bed in the hotel room was also silver, with a headboard that matched the control panel. The ceiling was studded with tiny lights meant to look like stars, and the walls were midnight blue. There was a lava lamp on a futuristic-looking desk at the side of the room. The wall-mounted television was made to look like a scanner screen with moulded plastic controls round it. She hadn't dared to look in the bathroom.

When Jade opened the curtains, which were also silver, she found herself looking out over the grey, cratered surface of the moon. "Do me a favour," she sighed.

She finally worked out how to raise the moonscape blind. But the view of the *Boscombe Heights Adventure Park* hotel's car park was hardly an improvement. Jade sighed and flopped down on the bed. She was just deciding that things couldn't get much worse when the countdown she'd started the control panel reached zero.

The room lights flashed on and off and a siren sounded, followed by the whoosh of rocket engines. The bed started to shake, and Jade leaped to her feet. The floor was absolutely still, but there was some mechanism making the bed move.

"We have lift off!" announced a deep voice with an obviously fake American accent. "Enjoy your trip... to the stars!"

"I see you're settling in," said a quieter voice.

McCain was standing in the connecting door. Jade could see his room looked very much like her own, but with a double bed.

"Great, isn't it?" he said.

Jade's reply was heavy with sarcasm. "Oh, it's just brilliant."

"Won't be for long. I expect those goons will have gone by tomorrow and we can move on. Best not try to call anyone, though." He nodded at a space-age telephone hanging by the bed. "They may have tapped the phones."

"Who may have?" demanded Jade. "Who are these people? You said you owe them money or something, but they've got cars and helicopters and guns, and now you think they're tapping the phones. What's going on?"

"I'll tell you soon enough, I promise. Let's make sure we're safe and in the clear, and then we can contact your father, all right?"

"And what about Rich?"

"Let's hope he got away from them. He'll get in touch with your dad too, won't he? Through Ardman, as soon as he can."

"So why don't we call Ardman now?" said Jade. "If anyone can sort this mess out, it's Ardman."

"When we're safe," repeated McCain. "You wait here. Keep your head down. Get room service to send up a drink and something to eat. You can watch TV."

"TV?!"

"Might be a repeat of *Star Trek*."

"Oh very funny. And what will you be doing?"

"Thought I'd have a quick look round. See if I can spot anyone looking for us."

"And what if they spot *you*?"

McCain smiled. "Trust me, they won't."

It was the toilet paper that finally did it. There wasn't a roll fixed to the bathroom wall, or even a dispenser with separate sheets. There was a button. The toilet itself looked like a metal mushroom, and the bath was circular with a shower shaped like a spaceship hanging over it and curtains patterned with stars and planets.

And a button for the loo paper. When Jade pressed it there was a sound like tickertape printing, and tissue paper juddered slowly out from a narrow slot in the wall. The paper was printed with lines and nodes so it looked like a circuit board. Jade was so astonished, she kept holding the button and before long the paper was piling up on the floor.

"Gordon Bennett," she said, and let go of the button. "Right – that's it. That. Is. It."

She was going to look for McCain, and she was

going to find Rich. If she couldn't find them, she was calling Ardman. She'd been thinking about what McCain had said, and the more she thought about it, the less sense it made. They'd already spoken to Halford on the phone, so Ardman would know by now that she and Rich were with McCain and in trouble. She had to tell him where they were.

She had been thinking about the woman who'd chased her through the haunted house too. Over and over again, she replayed in her mind the moment when the woman found her in the graveyard. The way she'd reached into her jacket for her gun. Except, she hadn't, had she? She'd taken out something else. Not her gun, which Jade had seen clearly in a holster on the other side, but a leather wallet. What was that all about?

"Believe me, you're in big trouble" – that was what the woman had said. But the more Jade thought about it, the less it sounded like a threat, and the more it sounded like a simple statement of fact...

Yet McCain said the woman was one of the bad guys, and Halford had told them they could trust McCain...

One thing was for sure, Jade knew she wasn't going to work it out sitting in her room with the scanner television, rocket control panel, lava lamp and tickertape loo paper. She needed some air and – like she'd told the receptionist – some space. She thought about calling Ardman, but decided against it. Not until she knew what was really going on. In any case, McCain might have had the phone barred, and he'd know if she'd used it if he checked their account on the scanner television. And maybe it really was tapped…

So she let herself out of the room, slipped the plastic key card (silver, of course) into her pocket, and headed down to the hotel restaurant and bar. She was starving and she was thirsty, and if McCain could wander around and – probably – get himself a drink, then so could she.

The main hotel bar wasn't space-themed. It was a pirate ship. With lunch being served, it was busy with families who'd just arrived and were looking forward to spending the afternoon in the theme park, or with parents who'd escaped from their older children and left them to enjoy the park on their own.

The bar area was raised up on the deck of the enormous ship. The waiters and waitresses wore striped shirts and eye patches. The plates were shaped like fish. Skull and crossbones flags hung everywhere.

Jade kept looking round as she wandered through the bar. She could see an empty booth in a shadowy area at the edge of the room. She sat down and examined the menu. The choice varied from *Pirates Platter* and *Smugglers Surprise* to *Captain Flints Fish and Chips*. To Jade's disgust, none of the dishes came with apostrophes.

"Get you anything, me hearty?" asked a broad, West-Country voice, belonging to a tall, thin pirate who had a toy parrot stuck to his shoulder.

"Orange juice," said Jade. "And do you do sandwiches?"

The pirate waiter leaned forward to turn over the menu. His parrot flopped alarmingly. He pointed to a section titled *Buccaneers Baps*.

"Close enough," Jade decided. "I'll have tuna and sweetcorn."

"You want fries with that?"

Jade glared at him. "Did I ask for fries with that?"

"No," the pirate decided, his accent abandoned for a home counties drawl. "Good point. Just the tuna and sweetcorn bap then and orange juice." He scribbled a note on his pirate pad with a fake quill pen and departed.

While she waited for her lunch, Jade looked round at the other people in the bar. She couldn't see the woman who'd chased her or anyone else who looked suspicious. No men in suits and dark glasses. Wasn't that what the Secret Service wore? She'd read somewhere – or Rich or her dad had told her – that they wore dark glasses so people couldn't tell if an agent was watching them.

An agent. Jade went cold at the thought. Her orange juice arrived with another "me hearty!" but she barely noticed. The woman in the graveyard had been warning her she was in trouble, and she had tried to show Jade something, just before McCain decked her with the shovel. A leather wallet. Like the FBI or CIA flipped open in the movies to show their badges.

She was in trouble all right. She just didn't know what sort.

The waiter risked a grin as he delivered a large bap spilling tuna mayonnaise and sweetcorn over a handful of crisps and a brave attempt at a side salad.

"Thanks," said Jade, "me hearty," she added. She

gave him her room number to charge the meal to, and he jotted it down.

"Anything else?"

"Just some peace and quiet."

The pirate laughed. "You'll be lucky. They'll be starting the sea shanties in a minute."

Jade hoped he was joking, but was afraid he wasn't. She could see a pirate with an accordion limbering up at the bar together with a large woman with dangly earrings and a striped shirt that didn't do her any favours. Jade sighed, and was about to start her lunch when she saw a man standing further along the bar. He was wearing a dark suit.

As she watched, he turned slightly, picking up a glass of Coke. He had black hair slicked back from his forehead, and a pale brown face that was lined like old stone. He looked familiar, but Jade didn't know if he was one of the men who'd been following them in the cars or the helicopter. The suit was the wrong style and shade.

Jade was still trying to work out where she'd seen him before, when McCain walked into the bar. He looked round, obviously checking there was no one there he wanted to avoid. Instinctively, Jade shrank back into the booth, hoping he hadn't seen her.

When she edged along and looked round the low wooden wall, she saw that McCain was walking up the gangplank to the bar. Further along, the man was sipping his Coke. He had turned, and she could see a pale scar running from above his left eye down the length of his cheek. Seeing it made Jade realise where she'd seen him before – at the farm. He'd been looking for them – one of the first men to come after them, before the helicopter.

Jade stood up. The man would see McCain any moment. She didn't have time to get to him – should she shout a warning? Would the man with the scar try anything in a crowded bar?

It was too late. The man with the scar had seen McCain. He set down his drink on the bar and stood up. He walked slowly and deliberately towards McCain, who had stopped dead in his tracks. The man with the scar smiled and reached out, enfolding McCain in an affectionate bear hug.

Jade ducked back into the booth, startled and afraid. McCain and the scarred man *knew* each other. She had the sudden, cold feeling she'd been tricked all along. The woman with the official badge – if that's what it was – had tried to warn her. The man who'd been chasing McCain and trying to kill him was actually his friend. It was all a trap of some sort. A set-up. And it looked like Jade and Rich had fallen right into it.

The good news – maybe the only good news – was that McCain didn't know Jade was on to him. She could slip away and find a phone. Or, she thought, she could try to get close enough to hear what the two men were saying. Maybe McCain had been telling the truth and was now trying to cut a deal of some sort... But she didn't really believe that.

She would have to go past the bar to get out anyway. Jade made her decision, and got slowly and carefully to her feet. She looked across to the bar, and found the pirate waiter who had served her standing there with another orange juice.

"Free refill," he said. "It's Hearty Hour."

"Thanks." Jade took the orange juice and drank it straight down. She didn't know when she'd next get a drink, and the vitamin C would do her good. She gave the empty glass back to the waiter.

"Sorry," he said quietly. Even his parrot looked sad as he turned and walked away.

Jade watched him go, puzzled. But she had enough to worry about already, so she made her way cautiously towards the bar. She found a spot out of sight round the prow of the 'boat'. It wasn't ideal, but she was confident that neither of the men could see her, and she could hear odd snatches of their conversation.

"Not yet," McCain was saying. "But it won't be long. He knows where it is. He put it there."

The other man's voice was quieter and he was facing away. Jade could hear almost nothing of what he said.

"Chance must return soon," said McCain. Someone laughed nearby, and Jade missed the rest of what he said. "…Didn't think we could force him to tell us," McCain was saying when the noise died down again, "but now we have something I expect he wants very badly. He'll tell us all right."

It sounded like they were hoping to get something from her dad, Jade thought. McCain had hoped to find him at the cottage. Hoped to ask her father for something. Now he had a way to force Dad to tell him what he wanted to know.

She was feeling suddenly light-headed and woozy. She felt even worse as she realised that the 'something' McCain thought he had to bargain with was *her*. It was definitely time to be going, but her legs weren't working. In fact, she was having trouble getting up. She grabbed the nearest thing to force herself off the bar stool. It was a sign propped up against the bar:

'Hearty Hour – Free Refills: 6:30-7:30 every nite'

She felt the last of her energy draining away. It wasn't Hearty Hour at all. The orange juice refill wasn't free – someone had paid for it. McCain must have seen her when he came in, and guessed she was on to him when Jade tried to hide in the booth. The waiter had said he was sorry – and he was sorry because he'd seen what McCain put in the drink. A pill, a liquid… The waiter was in on it. Probably bribed.

But that didn't matter. What *did* matter was that Jade had to get out of the bar and find somewhere to hide so she could sleep off whatever the drug was.

She tried to put one foot in front of the other. Shuffling along. Then came the crash of a falling chair.

Somewhere a hundred miles away a woman was singing *A Pirate's Life for Me*, accompanied by an accordion. Jade almost laughed. The fat lady was singing, and as the floor rushed towards her she knew it was all over.

"It's all right, no worries. I'll get her." McCain's

voice sounded as though it was filtered through soggy cotton wool. Jade felt his hands on her shoulders, lifting her up.

"She's just dead on her feet."

Then nothing.

9

Although few of the people who worked with Hilary Ardman knew it, he'd been a good field agent once. But that was years ago. Now he was responsible for a department that didn't officially exist and that reported directly to the British Cabinet's emergency committee known as COBRA.

If there was a security matter within the British Isles that the police, Special Branch, or MI5 didn't want to handle – or for some reason couldn't be seen to be involved with – then Ardman's group was called in.

If there was a 'problem' overseas that the armed forces or MI6 couldn't handle, then it went to Ardman.

He had a small team of carefully chosen operatives, but the power to call on help from any of the other 'services' he needed. Some of those services resented Ardman's power and remit. But most of them were only too glad to help – the better Ardman did his job, the more likely he was to keep it. And when all was said and done, the alternative didn't bear thinking about – no one wanted such a powerful agency to be run by anyone but Hilary Ardman.

No one apart from terrorists, organised criminals, smugglers and warlords, anyway.

Over the years, Ardman had faced down trained gunmen, got the better of bombers and madmen, argued vehemently with Prime Ministers and the Joint Chiefs of Staff. He had calmly and efficiently got his own way in meetings and situations where other senior staff had been looking pale and feeling sick.

Now, as he stood in a small, unmarked room in Heathrow's Terminal 5, Ardman reflected on some of those meetings and encounters. And he decided that he had never been as apprehensive as he was at that moment. The flight had landed, the passengers were disembarking. Shortly, the man Ardman had sent to sort out a 'problem' in South America would be walking towards him. And Ardman had bad news for him.

The flight was late as most flights were. John Chance didn't care. He had fallen asleep as soon as the wheels left the ground in Rio, and he didn't really wake up until they touched the tarmac in London.

Occasionally, his eyes had flicked open, on a sort of autopilot of their own. Whenever anyone brushed by or there was a sudden noise, or a slight change in the air temperature or a bump of turbulence. Whenever the slightest thing happened that might signify danger, John Chance opened his eyes, scanned the plane for any problems, and then switched off totally once more.

Before boarding the flight, he had been awake for seventy-two hours, give or take a few minutes. But it had been worth it. He'd done his job, earned the reluctant thanks of a local army officer, and made the world a better, safer place. Probably. Now he was going home for a rest.

Even a couple of years ago, Chance wouldn't have thought of himself as a homebody. He wouldn't have considered settling down, and any thoughts of a family were right out. But just as circumstances changed quickly in his professional life, so they'd changed quickly in his personal life too. Suddenly he had found himself a father of teenage twins. It had changed his perspective. It earned his – initially – reluctant thanks. And it made John Chance's world a better place. Definitely.

So far, it had to be said, his family world had not been a safer place. His children seemed to have inherited Chance's own knack of getting into trouble. Luckily they also seemed to have his knack of getting out of it again. But maybe that was luck, and Chance knew that you only had to be unlucky once. He was looking forward to going home, and seeing his children, and forgetting all about how terrible and unsafe the world could actually be...

He watched with tight-lipped amusement as people hurried to stand up and grab their bags as soon as the plane stopped. For all their impatience, they might gain a couple of minutes at most. Chance waited till the people started to move before joining the crush. He only had a small holdall. A scheduled flight was the quickest and cheapest way for him to travel, and his other luggage would be sent back by a different, more secure route.

A child in front of Chance slipped and fell as someone jostled her. Chance caught her arm with his free hand – automatically, without thinking. He pulled her back to her feet and smiled at her. The girl's mother muttered a thank you, her surprise at the speed of his reaction evident in her eyes. Yes, Chance was looking forward to seeing the twins again. They'd be in school now of course, but he'd ring and leave a message at the cottage as soon as he was off the plane.

When everyone else headed for passport control, Chance stopped at an unmarked door, and knocked. The window in the door was opaque, but he knew that someone was watching from the other side of the one-way glass.

Sure enough the door opened, and Chance handed the uniformed official his passport.

The man barely glanced at it. "Welcome home, sir," he said. "Mr Ardman is waiting for you."

Chance frowned. His mission had not been *that* important, and there were no problems. He hadn't expected to see Ardman until after the weekend for a routine debriefing. But he could see a tall, lean man with thinning dark hair standing at the back of the room. Chance felt his stomach tighten as the official closed and locked the door, and then left the room by a side exit.

"I'm sorry," said Ardman.

Chance stared back at him through cold, blue, unblinking eyes. His voice was every bit as cold and flint-hard. "Just tell me."

Ardman nodded. "Mark Darrow has your daughter."

The world was white. There was a breeze. Even before she opened her eyes, Jade could tell there was something odd about the quality of the light. Like when you know it's snowed even before you open the curtains. But it was too warm for that – despite the cool of the breeze, it was hot.

She opened her eyes. Thin, silk curtains hid the outside world from her. They rippled and shimmered round the bed. The sheets were also white silk. The pillow was the softest she'd ever rested her head on.

Jade snuggled down into the luxurious softness of it all, and closed her eyes again.

Then, suddenly, she was awake. Where was she? What was going on? She remembered the bar, the pirate waiter. McCain and the drugged drink – falling... Was she in another room in the hotel? Not Space Zone, obviously, but maybe Luxury Land?

Pushing the sheets aside, Jade saw she was still dressed in the same jogging bottoms and sweatshirt. She fought her way through the billowing silk curtains, and saw that someone had laid out a white silk dressing gown over the back of an ornate wooden chair. On the chair was a change of clothes – thin shirt, trousers, a headscarf... All white. All silk.

She ignored the clothes and walked slowly round the bedroom. Everything was pale. The walls were painted white; the floor was pale marble and warm under her bare feet. The furniture was light wood with gilt handles and trimmings. The breeze was coming from vents close to the floor.

Through an archway was a small bathroom, almost filled by a large sunken bath. It was already full of foaming water. Jade dipped her toe in, and found it was pleasantly cool. She was tempted to take a bath in it straight away, but she wanted to know where she was first. Once – if – she found she was safe, then she'd allow herself to relax and have a bath. But not before.

Her trainers were under the chair, and Jade pulled them on to her bare feet.

There was a large wooden door with a gold handle.

There was no keyhole, but she expected the door to be bolted. In fact, it opened easily.

Outside was a wide corridor. The walls and floor matched the bedroom. There were other doors, but Jade followed the passageway. She didn't see anyone or hear any signs of life.

The passage ended in a flight of steps – leading both up and down. Jade could feel the heat coming up from below, so she decided to try upstairs first. The steps were rough stone and the walls seemed to be textured with sand.

Jade walked carefully and quietly. The stairs turned sharply, and she could feel the warmth, could see the sunlight filtering down from above. The steps emerged on to a vast, flat roof. The sky above was azure blue and the sun beat down so hard that Jade had to screw up her eyes against the glare.

As she gradually got used to the light, she made out tall palm trees in large earthenware pots. Moving closer, she could see that the trees were swaying gently over the edge of a massive swimming pool. The water was as blue and clear as the sky.

Beyond the pool, there were steps up to a raised area of the roof. A low wall round the section where Jade was standing meant she could see nothing but the sky. They must be high up. There was no wall round the upper level, so Jade climbed the steps.

The floor of the upper area was covered in dark asphalt. The area was square, with a large circle painted in white and marked off round the edge. It was, Jade realised, a helicopter landing pad.

But that was not what made her gasp with astonishment. From up here, she could see out over the surrounding area.

She stood and stared, the warm breeze catching her hair and tugging at her sweatshirt. She was not as high up as she had thought. The reason she could see nothing was because there *was* nothing to see. There were no buildings and no trees, as far as Jade could see.

Just sand. Rolling, golden sand stretched to the horizon in every direction. Jade was standing alone on the roof of the only building in a vast, empty desert.

10

The helicopter flew Rich and Halford down to London. The American agents Chuck White and Kate Hunter left in a fast car, together with two other dark-suited Americans.

As the helicopter lifted from the car park, Rich looked down on the huge *Boscombe Heights Adventure Park*. The rides were like toys, the people tiny as ants. He could see uniformed local police working their way through the crowds and knew they were showing photographs of Jade and McCain – *Darrow* – to everyone.

The picture of Jade was one that Ardman's people had sent through – goodness knew how they'd got it, but it looked like her passport photo. The picture of Darrow was a scanned and enhanced copy of the photo Rich had brought with him, carefully cropped so it showed only Darrow and not his SAS colleagues.

He hated to leave, but Rich knew that by now Darrow was probably miles away, and Jade with him. If they were still at the theme park, then the police had more chance of finding them than Rich and Halford.

Even so, he was in a sullen mood all the way down to London. Halford soon gave up trying to make conversation, which was difficult enough anyway in the noisy cabin. It wasn't until the helicopter touched down in the grounds of a country house, just outside the M25 on the very outskirts of London, that Rich began to feel better.

The helicopter had barely touched down, and was still bouncing slightly on its wheels when the door was hauled open and a man leaned into the cabin.

"Dad!" exclaimed Rich.

His father smiled. But Rich could see the concern and anger in John Chance's eyes. "What the hell have you and Jade got yourselves into this time?" he demanded.

"Sorry about the location," said Ardman. "Speed is of the essence and there was room to land a helicopter on the lawn. Algernon's away for the week, so we have the place to ourselves."

He did not explain who Algernon was – or even if he knew he had unexpected guests. No one asked.

They were in a large library in the west wing of the stately home. Dark wooden bookcases lined the walls, filled with leather-bound volumes. Almost all the furniture had been removed or pushed to the sides of the room, and replaced with a modern horseshoe-shaped desk made up of sections. One side of the horseshoe was covered with computer and monitoring equipment, while the other looked like a communications exchange with radios, telephones, a fax machine and a video-conferencing set-up.

The end of the horseshoe was piled with papers and documents. A flipchart stood to one side, with a list on it: "Ports, Airports, Harbours, Chunnel, Rail, Motorway network cameras, Radar intercept, Sat-intel…" Each and every item had a tick against it.

Inside the middle of the horseshoe, two men wheeled rapidly about on office chairs. They moved swiftly and efficiently between computers and phones, monitors and keyboards.

"The big question is *why?*" Ardman went on. "Once we know that, everything else will fall into place."

"The big question is where's Jade?" said Rich.

"With respect, that's not the big question."

"But—"

Rich felt his dad's hand on his shoulder. "Ardman's right. Knowing where Jade is won't tell us what's going on or what Darrow wants. But if we work out what he's after, that will tell us where he's gone."

"Probably," Halford growled.

Ardman sighed. "Actually, Rich is probably right," he admitted. "The answers to any questions at all right now would be helpful."

"So what do we know?" Chance demanded.

"Not a lot." Ardman counted the points off on his fingers as he spoke. "We know that Darrow went to your cottage looking for you. He claimed he was being chased and in trouble, and that does appear to be born out by events." He looked at Rich for confirmation.

Rich nodded. "The Americans were after him, and us, but not until later according to Chuck. There was someone after him right from the start, at the cottage.

They had guns, cars…" He shrugged. "I didn't really see who they were though. And Darrow wasn't really happy talking about it."

"So we know he's in trouble and he comes to *you*." Ardman pointed at Chance. "But we also know that before he came looking for you, he called on Ferdy McCain – the real McCain."

"And murdered him," said Halford quietly.

"With respect, we cannot know that for sure. It may be that these mysterious pursuers killed McCain after Darrow saw him, or maybe Darrow was never there. Although Goddard tells me the local police did get a description that matches our friend Mr Darrow from one of the neighbours. He was asking after McCain the day before."

"Either way," Chance cut in, "Darrow came looking for me. And when I wasn't there, he pretended to be McCain, presumably because if Rich and Jade contacted me I'd be more likely to talk to McCain than to Darrow. Which is certainly true. Ferdy was a good bloke," he added quietly.

"But they can't contact you, so Darrow takes them with him. Probably as leverage to get you to meet him later."

"But he still has Jade," said Chance. "And he wants something from me. But what?"

"I'm afraid there may be only one way to find out," said Ardman. "Are you all set up for the cottage, Pete?" he called across to one of the two technicians.

"Phone will divert here, sir," Pete confirmed. He ran a hand over his very short hair. "Alan's hacked into the traffic camera on the routes in and out of the village, and Goddard's coordinating with the local coppers so they'll keep a low profile."

"We've got satellite coverage coming up in a few minutes. The French security services were kind enough to lend us one of their birds that has a pretty good angle at the moment." Alan added.

"That was unusually kind of them," said Chance.

"Oh, they don't know about it," said Alan, grinning. "They think it's over Dinard keeping an eye on the nuclear power station there. But actually they're watching footage from last month. Let's just hope the weather is roughly the same for a bit, otherwise they might realise they've got a bit of a technical fault."

"Too much information, thank you," said Ardman. "I don't need or want to know the details."

"Can't the Americans help?" asked Rich. "They

must have satellites you could use, and the CIA want Darrow."

Ardman spoke slowly and carefully. "There are a few misconceptions in your statement, young man. First, the Americans would tell us that they don't have satellites looking down on Britain, as we are their favourite allies."

Behind him Pete cleared his throat, and Alan shuffled his feet.

Ardman glared at them. "That is what they would *tell* us," he said sternly. "And second, I doubt very much if the CIA know that there are American agents looking for Mark Darrow. Mr White and Miss Hunter and their colleagues are with a different American security service."

"The FBI?" asked Rich.

"They don't operate outside the US," Halford told him.

Before Rich could say anything else, Ardman went on: "The important thing is that we have your cottage fully covered, John. Darrow wants something, and he knows you'll talk to him if he's got Jade. So when he makes contact, we'll be ready and waiting. And then, once we have more information, we can decide what action to take."

"The most important thing is that we get Jade back safe and sound," said Chance.

"I agree that is currently the way it looks," said Ardman.

"What do you mean, *currently*?" demanded Rich. "What could change that? Jade's always going to be the most important thing. Isn't she, Dad?" He turned to his father, expecting him to agree immediately.

But instead, John Chance looked to Ardman.

"However much we want to get your sister back," Ardman said, "our priorities may have to change when we find out what it is that Darrow wants in return."

As she walked slowly back down the stairs, Jade felt numb. She was in the middle of nowhere. There wasn't even a road that she could see through the desert. The building she was in – a villa or whatever it was – looked very big from the size of the roof, and it was several storeys high. There were large parts she had still not explored.

But what – and who – would she find? So far there was no sign of life. Nothing to indicate there was anyone else here at all. Yet someone had brought Jade here, someone had taken her shoes off and put her to bed, leaving fresh clothes and a bath full of water that was still warm...

Without really thinking about it, Jade kept going down the stairs. It took her a moment to realise she'd passed the floor where her room was, but she decided to keep going and see what was on the floor below.

The answer was: nothing. The stairs ended in a small, empty, whitewashed room. There was a thin layer of sand on the floor. Maybe it was a storage area, except there was nothing stored down here. A single, bare, electric bulb cast a harsh light over the walls and floor. Jade turned to go back up the stairs.

Then she stopped. The sand by one wall was scuffed about, as if someone had walked through it. But it was so close to the wall that no one could have done. If it really was a wall...

Jade ran her hand over the rough stonework. She couldn't feel anything out of the ordinary. She pushed, and the wall was unforgiving. She moved along, pressing at another point. Was it her imagination, or did the surface move under her hand, just the tiniest amount? She put her shoulder to the wall and leaned – and while it didn't appear to move, she did hear a rough scraping sound of stone rubbing on sand...

It took her several minutes of experimentation to find exactly the right point to apply pressure. Then the mechanism activated, and the whole wall hinged open like a door. Cautiously, Jade stepped through. She didn't dare close the door behind her – she might need to retreat in a hurry, and she didn't want to have to spend forever finding the release mechanism on the other side.

At first she thought the hidden door led nowhere. She was just in another room – long and narrow, but still quite small. Then she saw her reflection looking back at her from the other end, and realised the whole of the far wall was actually a window.

She approached slowly and warily, in case there was anyone on the other side, but all she could see was a vaulted stone roof. Until she got closer, and realised that the window was high above the enormous chamber below. She was in some sort of observation gallery. Jade looked down into the chamber.

She could hear nothing; the glass must be incredibly thick. There were several people in the chamber – they looked like scientists and technicians in white lab coats, which contrasted with their dark skin. One was working at a table almost directly below Jade, putting test tubes into a centrifuge. Another was at a computer. He turned and gestured to one of his colleagues.

Further into the chamber, a woman pushed her arms into thick plastic sheaths and gloves that reached into a sealed glass cabinet. Whatever was inside, she didn't want to handle it directly.

The chamber must stretch right under the building. Jade could just make out more white-coated figures in the distance. Whatever they were doing, there was a seriousness and professionalism that frightened Jade. She was witnessing something she wasn't supposed to see. The situation she was in didn't offer her many advantages, but maybe this was one. So long as they didn't find out what she knew, Jade thought, that gave her an edge.

Except that she didn't know who 'they' were, and she had no idea what it was that she was looking at. The scientists and technicians could be testing a satellite, synthesising drugs, or baking a cake. She guessed that baking a cake was pretty unlikely, but the options were still too numerous to be helpful.

Jade backed slowly out of the observation gallery, pushed the secret door closed, and started back up the stairs.

There was a lot more of the building still to explore. But she needed to think. If she went the other way down the passage from her room, she was confident she would find people – maybe a kitchen, possibly guards. But for the moment no one knew she was out of her room, or even awake. She had spotted no cameras, and was sure no one had seen or heard her.

Since she obviously wasn't going anywhere, Jade decided she might as well have that bath and consider what to do next.

Soaking in the luxuriously cool water, Jade decided on her plan of action. She needed to know as much as possible about the place, and she needed to keep the extent of her knowledge secret. Eventually someone would come to find her, and the more she knew by then the more she might glean from them.

And you never knew. If there was a secret underground laboratory, then maybe there was transport of some sort, or a telephone that she could use to call Ardman or Halford.

She was glad of the bath, and felt a lot better for it. But she didn't want to waste any more time. Whoever had left her here – McCain, or the man with the scar, or someone else – might think it was safe enough to leave her unattended in a building in the middle of the desert, but Jade was determined to prove them wrong.

She dried herself quickly, and slipped on the white silk dressing gown. She was rubbing at her hair with the towel as she walked briskly back into the bedroom. But the clothes that had been left on the chair were no longer there. They were lying neatly on the dressing table nearby.

Put there, Jade realised, by the man who was now sitting in the chair. Watching her.

He was wearing white robes and an Arab headdress. His face was as wrinkled as a prune – even more so as he smiled up at Jade. His eyes were deep and dark, and a neatly trimmed grey beard clung to his chin. As he shifted slightly in the chair to see Jade better, she caught sight of the curved sword hanging at his side.

"Who the hell are you?" Jade demanded. "And why am I here – wherever *here* is?"

The man inclined his head slightly, as if Jade had paid him a compliment. "My name is Ali," he said, his accented voice deep and rich. "I am honoured to have you as my guest, Miss Chance."

"Believe me, the honour is all yours."

The man pressed his hands together, fingertip to fingertip. "I am sorry that you have to stay here for a short while. But if all goes well, you will be able to leave in a very few days."

"You reckon?"

"In the mean time, please – my humble house is your home. You may swim in the pool, sunbathe in the roof garden, order what you like from my kitchens… though I warn you they are not as well stocked as they might be. You may walk outside the house if you wish, but I would caution you not to go too far as the sun is hot and the desert is unforgiving."

"Is that a threat?"

Ali shook his head. "A statement. If you want to walk out into the desert and die of heat and dehydration no one will stop you, and no one will go looking. Or if you prefer there is a snooker hall, and a small cinema with many American DVDs." He smiled apologetically. "No alcohol, I'm afraid."

"I don't drink."

"Then that will not be a problem."

"And I'm not staying. You can get a helicopter here right now and send me home."

"I'm sorry." Ali stood up. "I can make your stay here

as pleasant as possible, but you will not be going home just yet. Soon, I hope, but not yet." He walked to the door, and paused for a moment.

"Take comfort in the fact that, albeit indirectly, you are doing my country the very greatest service just by being here. My people will be truly grateful."

He pressed his hands together again, bowed, and left.

11

The waiting was the worst. Rich hated it. He felt so useless and just wished there was something he could do, but he knew that Ardman's team was doing everything they could.

There was actually lots to do. And though playing billiards with Dad in the snooker room of the enormous mansion did take his mind of things for a while, Rich felt guilty when he remembered why they were there. And as well as being worried about Jade, he missed her.

"What if Darrow doesn't call?" Rich asked Chance as they played.

"He will."

Chance sounded confident. But Rich had noticed

the slight hesitation before his father answered him. "Course he will," said Rich quietly. "I mean, he has to, doesn't he."

The absent Algernon had been good enough to leave his cook and some of his staff behind, so there was no shortage of good food or people to get it. But Rich didn't feel hungry and he spent most of his time sitting at the back of the library watching Alan and Pete laughing and joking and checking their equipment. Neither of them seemed to sleep, and they ate a constant selection of sandwiches and snacks washed down with a never-ending stream of coffee.

The phones rang frequently, and whenever they did, Rich held his breath until it was obvious that the call wasn't from Darrow.

He barely slept that night. His bed was an ancient four-poster with heavy drapes tied back from the sides, and sheets and blankets rather than a duvet. It was unfamiliar and uncomfortable, and Rich was so tired he couldn't get to sleep. Several times he almost drifted off, his eyes closing and his mind clearing. Then he'd jolt awake again as he thought of Jade or heard an owl in the grounds outside.

The call came the next morning. Rich and Chance were walking in the extensive grounds, but keeping close to the house. Pete had routed the cottage phone to Chance's mobile. Somehow, Rich knew as soon as it rang that this was it.

Chance checked the number of the incoming call before answering. He looked at Rich, and Rich could see the sudden anger and determination in his dad's eyes. Then Chance was running back towards the house. Rich guessed he was leaving it as long as he dared before answering. Pete and Alan would already know the call was from the cottage number – a reroute – and be tracing it.

Like Rich, they'd all be hoping it wasn't just an innocent call from a friend or a double-glazing sales rep.

Rich didn't hear the start of the conversation, but as soon as they entered the library he could hear a voice he recognised coming through the speakers. The man who had told Rich he was Ferdy McCain – the man who now had Jade. Mark Darrow.

"…and I'm sure you have lots of friends with you, maybe even the resourceful Rich. The equally resourceful Jade is…" the voice hesitated. "Well, let's just say she's safe."

"She had better be," Chance growled into the phone. His voice too was amplified through the speakers.

"Oh she's having the time of her life. Let's just hope it isn't the *last* time of her life, eh?"

Rich wanted to grab the phone and yell down it, but he knew it would do no good. He saw his father's grip on the phone tighten.

"If anything happens to Jade," said Chance, menacingly calm, "you know you'll never sleep soundly again."

"I don't think I'll be the only one though, will I, John?" Darrow sounded upbeat and confident. In control. "So let's make sure it doesn't come to that."

"What do you want?"

Alan was working at the computers behind them. The monitor displayed a map of the world. A series of numbers flashed across it, ever changing. The map was slowly zooming in…

"I want your help, simple as that. I came to find you, John, and you weren't there. I was in a hurry, in trouble. I had to improvise."

"You didn't have to take my children."

"I suppose I could have left them there to get shot."

"You didn't have to take them hostage."

"Like I said, I need your help. And with Jade as my guest, I can be sure of getting it. Right?"

The map on the monitor showed Britain. It zoomed in on the location of the Chance's cottage. Numbers sped across the screen, and a line appeared from the cottage heading off to the east. Alan moved his mouse, and the image panned across, following the line. It got as far as London, then headed off again in another direction.

"Cutouts and reroutes," said Alan quietly.

Ardman nodded. "Do what you can," he mouthed.

"I'm in a bit of trouble," Darrow was saying.

"You're telling me," Chance retorted.

"No, really. You see, I owe some people some money. Money they paid me for certain services, which in the event I was unable to provide."

"You mean someone else killed him first?"

"Please, let's not be unpleasant. And sarcasm doesn't help either, you know, John."

Chance's jaw tightened. "Just tell me what you want, Darrow."

There was a pause before Darrow continued. "You remember when we were out in Iraq back in 1990, John? You, me, Ferdy and Dex."

"Ferdy's dead."

"Yeah. Shame that. I thought he might be able to help me, but it turns out you're the only one. He said even Dex couldn't tell me what I need to know. I was hoping not to have to come and find you, John. Ferdy was always so much more amenable."

"Is that why you killed him?"

"Oh, please." Darrow sounded outraged. "I killed him because he came at me with a hammer."

"Probably because he realised you were going to shoot him anyway."

"Quite likely," Darrow agreed happily. "Now, let's get back to Iraq, shall we?"

The line on the map was over New York now. There it split into several lines that headed off in different directions. Alan threw up his hands in defeat, and moved aside to let Pete take over the computer.

"Is there any point to these reminiscences?"

"Indeed there is. You see, I had a little scheme going back then. Not much in the grand scale of things, but there's the principle of it too, I suppose."

"You have principles?"

Darrow seemed not to have heard the insult. "You remember I picked up a souvenir while I was out there. A small statue."

"I remember."

"That you deprived me of."

"We had to leave it behind. We had to leave just about everything behind. You were lucky we didn't leave *you* behind after you got yourself shot-up."

"Yes, that's true. But that statue's mine and I want it back."

"Yours? You stole it."

"Well, finders-keepers and all that. Anyhow, that's the deal. You hid that statue somewhere, or you left it in southern Iraq and now I need it so I can sell it and pay off my debts. Oh, I know it's been a while, but without knowing where it is and without a buyer lined up, it was more trouble than it was worth to try to find it, or to ask you to help. And I had other things to do to keep me busy and well paid. But now, well, things have changed. So here's the proposition: the statue in return for your daughter. Sounds like a good deal to me, John. Why don't I call back in one hour and you can tell me where it is, and I'll put Jade on a plane back home? Or something."

"Now, wait a minute," Chance snarled into the handset.

But the speakers relayed only static. Darrow had hung up.

The next hour was tense. Pete and Alan were trying desperately to trace the source of Darrow's call, but the best they could offer was that it originated "Maybe somewhere in the Middle East. Or North Africa. Or not."

Chance and Halford recounted the story of their mission in Iraq. Rich was fascinated, but he couldn't see how any of this connected to current events.

Ardman too had reservations. "I've read the file," he admitted. "After all, it's best to know as much as possible about the people you recruit to work for you. But there has to be more to it than Darrow's letting on."

"The statue?"

"Maybe." Ardman sucked in his cheeks as he considered. "If the man really needs money, why doesn't he just ask for money? Why is this statue so important to him? Or, given his rather special skills, why doesn't he just go and steal another one from some museum?"

"So the statue is important itself," said Halford.

"Maybe it really is a point of principle," Rich suggested. "Dad took the statue from him, now he wants it back."

"Bit petty," Alan put in.

"Is Darrow a petty person?" Ardman wondered.

Halford shook his head. "Practical and efficient. Vicious and nasty. He'd kill someone for the hell of it – in that sense he's petty. But for a principle? Tit-for-tat, after so long? No, I doubt it."

"It would be useful to know who he needs to pay off," said Chance thoughtfully. "Because it may be that's who is demanding this statue. Or maybe Darrow upset them by promising to get it and then he couldn't deliver."

"Maybe it's just a priceless ancient Iraqi artefact and he really is just after the dosh," Pete called across from his desk. He shrugged apologetically. "It's possible, isn't it?"

"I guess so," admitted Chance. "It didn't look like much, though it was very heavy. Back in 1990, Darrow was very keen to keep hold of it."

"Either way," Ardman decided, "if the statue is that important or valuable, then I don't think we want Darrow to have it."

"But what about Jade?" Rich blurted out.

Ardman smiled. "Oh, I don't mean we shouldn't agree to hand it over. In fact I think we *should*, and get your sister back safe and sound as soon as we can. But that doesn't mean that Darrow should get to *keep* the statue, does it?"

"Darrow will insist on dictating where the handover takes place," said Halford. "We can't plan ahead till we know that, and as soon as we do he'll have all the advantage."

Chance turned to Pete and Alan. "You say that call came from the Middle East."

"Might have done," admitted Alan. "It's possible. Maybe even probable."

Chance nodded. "In that case, and given that Darrow seems desperate to get this statue back as soon as he can, I think I know exactly where he'll suggest we do the exchange."

"How does that help?" asked Rich.

"It helps because we can do a bit of forward planning," said Ardman. "And I know just the people who can help."

12

"Don't do that," said Chance.

"Sorry." Rich had been nervously playing with the metal beetle he'd won on the Hook-a-Duck.

They were standing in the Iraqi desert, by the crumbled remains of a large village. Rich didn't know how many strings had been pulled to get them here, but he still couldn't quite believe that the day before he'd been in an English manor house, and now he was in *Iraq*. He was standing in the hot sand of one of the most dangerous countries on earth, about to take on an ex-SAS soldier in a deadly game of bluff...

Nervously, he gave the metal strip welded to the beetle's body one more press. Click-clack.

Chance sighed and turned slowly to glare at him.

"Sorry," said Rich again, stuffing the toy back into his pocket. "I was just mucking about."

"Well don't. It sounds like a gun being readied. Just like the bolt action of an old 2.2 rifle, or someone cocking a pistol."

"Really?"

"Plus," said Chance, "it's *really* irritating." He went back to examining the sand next to a ruined wall. "I brought you here to keep an eye on you, not so you could click-click-click at me all the time."

"Have you found it yet?" asked Rich, changing the subject.

Chance shook his head. "I'm sure this is the one. Of course, it was a long time ago, and there's no way of knowing if anyone else has found it already."

Rich looked around. "It doesn't look like there's been anyone here for years. You sure you've got the right building?"

"No. It was nearly twenty years ago, so I'm not sure about anything."

Almost as soon as he finished speaking, Chance gave a grunt of satisfaction and pulled a battered water bottle out of the sand.

"You left your water?" said Rich.

"Just the empty bottles." He pulled out a webbing belt and threw it aside.

Rich knelt to help, scrabbling beside his father in the sand and rubble. Straight away, he felt something hard in the soft sand. A smooth, rounded shape, covered in fabric. He scraped the sand away, Chance leaned across to help.

"Well done. I think you've got it."

Chance managed to get his hands under the rucksack that Rich had found and lift it clear of the sand. He set it down close by and dusted his hands together. Then he opened the top and lifted out the heavy statue inside.

"Is that it?" said Rich, unimpressed.

Chance nodded, putting it down beside the rucksack. The statue was earthenware or terracotta. Although it had worn so smooth that most of the details were lost, Rich could see that it was a stylised depiction of a lion rearing up on its hand legs.

"Were there lions here, then?" he asked.

Chance shrugged. "No idea. Maybe not, maybe that's why it's valuable. An ancient mystery, perhaps."

"Or a boring old statue. It's hideous."

"It's heavy, that's for sure," said Chance. He checked

his watch. "Good timing. Darrow will be here soon."

"Let's hope he's brought Jade with him."

Chance didn't answer. He had his mobile phone out and was working the buttons.

"You'll never get a signal out here," Rich pointed out.

"Not trying to. I'm just going to take a couple of pictures of our chum here."

Chance held his phone up and snapped the statue from the front, side and back. Then he tipped it over and took a picture of the base. It was flat, with a slight hollow. The edge was chipped and cracked.

"Careful you don't break it," said Rich.

Chance grinned. "There's an idea. Good one." He ran his thumbnail along the tiny crack and prised off a sliver.

"Here." He gave the tiny strip of pottery to Rich. "Stick that in your beetle and keep it safe. Might stop it making that stupid noise too."

Rich wedged the shard of pottery behind the metal strip that made the click-clack noise, and put the beetle back in his pocket.

"Just in time," he said. They could both hear the far off sound of a helicopter.

A short distance away, their own helicopter stood immobile on the sand. Its rotor blades drooped over the dark, bulbous body. Chance gave the pilot a thumbs-up, and the man returned the gesture.

"Will he tell Ardman we've found it?" asked Rich.

Chance shook his head. "Radio silence for now. Darrow could be monitoring the frequency. And so could the local security forces. We're not meant to be here, remember."

"I thought we liberated Iraq," said Rich.

"There are other, less generous interpretations. Not everyone in Iraq wanted to be liberated. And who knows what friends Darrow has made, or bribed out here. He's had a long time to plan this, whatever it is."

"OK, I get the picture." But Rich's words were swallowed up by the sound of the helicopter coming in to land.

Sand blew round them, kicked up by the helicopter's rotors. It stung Rich's face, and he pulled his headscarf round so only his eyes were exposed as he blinked away dust and sand.

The rotors slowed to a halt and the engine noise died away.

"Darrow's here, and we've found the statue," said

Chance loudly as he led Rich out into the open. "Let's see if he's brought Jade with him."

They stood with their hands raised as they waited for Darrow to emerge from the helicopter.

At last the door slid open, and a figure jumped to the ground. A figure dressed in white, with a silk headscarf rippling in the breeze.

Jade.

Rich almost ran to her, but Chance held him back and shook his head.

Darrow jumped down beside Jade, spreading his hands to show he wasn't holding a gun.

"So – we've got a deal, then. Do you have my statue?"

"It's nearby," Chance shouted back. "You send Jade over here and I'll get it."

"You get it, so I can see it. *Then* we'll exchange on open ground between the helicopters. Don't want you flying away with your family and not giving me what I want."

"As if," Chance muttered. "Rich, get the statue. Carefully."

As Rich went to get the statue from the ruined building, Chance walked slowly towards Darrow and Jade.

Jade made to run to him, but Darrow caught her arm and dragged her back.

"It's all right, Jade. Just be patient," Chance told her.

"You came unarmed, as we agreed?" Darrow asked. He licked his lips as he watched Rich carry the statue across to them.

The two groups stood about ten metres apart.

"So now what?" Jade asked.

"Now you come over to join us here, slowly," said Chance. He took the statue from Rich and started to walk slowly to Darrow. "And you can have your precious statue. Then we all go back to our helicopters and get out before the locals realise we were even here. And you be very careful," he said to Darrow, "because I know full well that you're not really unarmed."

Jade brushed her hand down Chance's arm as they passed, then she hurried to join Rich, enfolding him in a hug.

"And you're telling me you're not armed either?" said Darrow. Like Chance he was careful to keep the other group between him and their helicopter at all times.

"Oh, but I assure you I'm not."

"You'll forgive me if I don't believe you," said Darrow, taking the statue from Chance. "Thank you for this."

"Thank you for nothing," Chance told him.

Each of them backed slowly away – Chance towards Rich and Jade, Darrow towards his helicopter.

"You disappoint me, John," Darrow shouted across. "I thought you would try something."

Chance shook his head. "Not me," he shouted back.

Then he turned and enfolded both his children in a bear hug, diving for the ground and dragging them with him. Rich had been expecting it, but even so the breath was knocked out of him as they landed.

"Stay down!" ordered Chance.

Over his dad's shoulder, Rich could see the sand close to Darrow erupting. Darrow stared in disbelief as a broad-shouldered man in desert combat fatigues leaped from the hole where he had been buried in the sand and brought up his assault rifle.

Close to Darrow's helicopter, two more figures were struggling free of the desert ground. One of them leaped into position by the doorway, rifle aimed at the pilot.

A fourth figure pushed up through the sand on the other side of Darrow – a woman, also in combat gear and brandishing a rifle.

"That woman…" Jade gasped.

"Agent Kate Hunter," said Chance.

"She tried to rescue you from Darrow at *Boscombe Heights*," said Rich. "They're all CIA. Or something."

There was silence except for the sound of the wind as it whipped round the ruined buildings and fallen walls. Then Darrow laughed.

"You didn't disappoint me after all," he yelled. "I'm so glad."

"Really?" said Chuck White, the agent closest to Darrow.

"Really," said Darrow. "Because it means I don't have to feel at all guilty about this."

He flung himself to the ground. As he fell, rolling to protect the statue he was holding, Rich could see that Darrow had something else in his hand too. A small, black box.

"Detonator!" Chuck shouted, hurling himself to the ground.

Kate Hunter and the other agent followed suit. Only the American agent in the door of Darrow's helicopter remained standing, but not for long, as the helicopter exploded in a ball of fire. Black smoke billowed into the air.

Darrow ran for the cover of a broken wall, then ducked behind it.

"He can't go anywhere," said Rich.

"Unless he's got friends near by," said Chance. "Friends who will have seen the helicopter go up."

"A signal?" Jade gasped.

But Chance was on his feet, yelling at Chuck and his team. "Get under cover – quick as you can. Move it!"

They were already moving, heading for the nearest cover. Their own helicopter was too exposed, and too far away. They could all hear the noise now – above and beyond the sound of the burning helicopter. Engines, low and throbbing and getting louder and closer.

Black specs became dots, then blotches. Dark helicopters were stark against the blue sky as they swooped low over the ruined village. Sand kicked up all around Rich and Jade, as the deafening side-mounted machine guns fired.

Chuck and Hunter were in the clear, but the other

American agent was caught in the open. His body spasmed and juddered in a hail of gunfire before he dropped to the ground.

Close by, one of the helicopters lowered itself ponderously to the ground near where Darrow was sheltering. The rotors whipped up sand, spraying it across the landscape.

Then there was the whoosh of a rocket. A trail of fire streaked over the desert.

The helicopter that Rich, Chance and the American agents had arrived in was lifting off the ground. The pilot's face was grim as he leaned over the controls, desperate to get his craft off the ground and out of the kill zone.

The rocket hit the middle of the helicopter and smashed it sideways before the explosion blew it to smithereens. Rich ducked again, his hands over the back of his head as burning debris hurtled past him.

Only as the noise gradually faded did he look up. The helicopters were disappearing into the distance.

"You think they'll come back?" asked Jade, her voice shaking.

"I don't think they'll bother," said her father. "They

picked up Darrow and the statue, that's what they came for."

"I thought they were going to kill us," said Rich. He was trembling and it was an effort to stop his teeth from chattering.

Chuck White and Kate Hunter had joined them in time to hear Rich's comment.

"They *did* kill us," said Chuck, gesturing to the dead agent and the remains of the helicopter. "We're as stone cold dead as Hal and Mike."

"What do you mean?" said Jade.

"No helicopter, no communications," Chance told her.

"You've still got your guns," Rich told Chuck.

"You can't drink guns. We've got no water, precious little shelter, and it's a long way to the nearest oasis."

"Ardman will send someone," said Jade.

But Rich knew how difficult it had been for Ardman to get them here in the first place.

"Another helicopter mission will take time to arrange – probably days," Chance told them. "And that's if Ardman even realises there's a problem. Since we're maintaining radio silence, it'll be a while before anyone gets worried and longer before they decide to act."

"Are you telling me we're going to die of heat and thirst out here before anyone even knows there's a *problem*?" snapped Jade.

She was probably right, but Rich knew that losing their temper would do no good. "Hey, Jade," he said. "It's good to have you back, but, you know – chillax."

She stared at him. "You *what*?"

"Chillax," Rich repeated. "It means, like, chill out and relax."

Jade turned to her father. "We may never get out of this desert alive," she said seriously. "I realise that. But if we do, I want you to promise me something."

Chance looked anxious. "Depends what it is."

"If I ever – *ever* – use the word 'chillax'," said Jade, "I want you to shoot me." She pointed to the middle of her forehead. "Right here. OK?"

"OK," Chance agreed seriously.

"That's my sister," said Rich to Chuck and Kate, who were staring at Jade and Chance with open mouths. "Welcome back, Jade."

13

Chuck White and Kate Hunter hated to leave their dead colleagues behind. But they agreed with Chance that Darrow might return, or tip off the local Iraqi forces that there were undesirables in the area. Either way, they needed to move.

"The Pentagon might spot something on the satellite images for the area," said Chuck.

"Only if they're looking," said Chance. "And I'm guessing they don't know you guys are here, right?"

"True," said Chuck. "We don't usually let the Pentagon know what we're up to."

"Not unless we want everyone else to know as well," muttered Kate.

"So where are we going?" asked Rich.

"Nearest border is a hundred and fifty kilometres that way," said Chance, pointing into the sandy distance.

"Nice day for a walk," said Jade. "Bit hot though."

"It'll get hotter," her father told her. "We need to get some distance from here, then shelter from the heat of the day. We're better moving at night."

"He's been here before," said Rich. As they walked, he filled Jade in on what they knew about Darrow and the mysterious statue.

"So what happened to you?" Rich asked when he'd finished. His mouth was dry and he could feel his lips cracking. He was happy to stop talking for a while.

"I worked out McCain – Darrow – was up to no good. He met one of the guys who were after us. So I guess they weren't after us at all and it was all a set up to make us think he was in trouble."

"Guess so."

"But they realised I was on to them and drugged me. I woke up in this big villa place in the middle of the desert. Some Arab bloke lives there, I think. I assume he was guarding me for Darrow. Then Darrow arrived in a helicopter. And here I am."

There was precious little shelter and no sign of

water. Chance told them to watch for birds, as they might be heading towards a water hole. But there was no sign of life of any kind.

Eventually they slumped down on the side of a huge sandbank that afforded a little shade. Chuck had a canteen of water, and passed it round. They each took a small sip, each longed for more, and each knew they had to conserve the water for as long as possible.

"So, where are we heading?" asked Jade.

"East Araby," said Chance.

"Never heard of it," said Rich.

"It's a small, relatively insignificant country that borders Iraq, Kuwait and Saudi Arabia," Kate told them. She seemed about to say more, then caught Chuck's eye.

"The US has a large presence there," said Chance. "Big airbase, nuclear weapons if you believe the Russian propaganda." He glanced at Chuck. "That right?"

"Wouldn't know about the nukes," said Chuck in an offhand tone that suggested that actually he knew all about them. "But yes, it's our biggest base in the region. The country has no oil, so they'd be pretty badly off if it weren't for the aid we give them."

"In return for the airbase?" said Rich.

"Only place round here where we can keep our Stealth Bombers... according to rumour, anyway," said Chuck. He smiled. "The country's ruled by King Hassan. He's very pro-western. Very progressive. He's brought the country to the brink of democracy."

"Is that the place where there are going to be elections?" asked Jade. "There was a documentary or something, wasn't there?"

"That's right," said Kate. "There are elections due in the next month. It's a big thing. First country round here to embrace democracy."

"It's a brave man who gives up power," said Chance. "Let's hope it all goes smoothly."

"You mean it might not?" said Rich. "Don't tell me we're walking out of the desert and into a coup."

Chuck smiled. "Hassan is a powerful and well-respected man. What he says, goes. The military might not like it, but they'll accept it because Hassan is a hero to them too. So long as King Hassan is in charge and stays on as a ceremonial Head of State, they'll go along with it."

"You know a lot about this," said Chance quietly.

"I read widely," Chuck told him.

But Rich sensed there was more to it than that – an undercurrent of meaning that he was missing.

"Right, let's move on," said Chance. "It's getting cooler as evening approaches, and I'd like to cover another few miles before sunset."

The heat of the sand was seeping through Jade's trainers. Every step seemed to sink deeper into the hot desert so that it was like wading through treacle. Her eyes were half closed against the dazzling sun. They'd walked for so long that Jade could barely remember anything other than the heat, anything other than the effort of putting one foot in front of the other.

"Are we nearly there yet?" asked Rich in a whining kiddie voice.

Jade laughed despite herself. Or tried to. Her throat felt like it was clogged with sand. Every scorching breath was an effort.

They were climbing steadily. But the convex shape of the sand dune meant that the top was always out of sight. Jade had no idea how much further it was to the summit, but she did know that even then there would be another dune to climb. The desert stretched for ever in every direction – just like the view from Ali's villa, only this time there was no swimming pool in the middle of it.

The others stopped for a breather, but Jade didn't notice. With her eyes screwed almost shut, lashes flecked with sand, she just kept walking. She vaguely heard Rich calling after her, but now she was at the top, looking down into a valley below.

A valley of unbroken, baking sand.

Except…

There was something at the base of the dune. A dark shape, a patch of shade. Relief from the sun. She stood staring down at it, trying to work out what it was. Could it be a dark patch of water? Or just discoloured sand? The remains of a fire? What?

Chance struggled up behind her. "We're at the top," he said, his voice a dry croak. "We'll walk along the ridge. Makes us easier to see, but it means we can see ahead too."

Jade just pointed. She wasn't sure her voice would work, but she tried: "What's that?"

Chance shaded his eyes from the sun. "Not sure…" There was a note of hope in his voice. "Got to be worth a look, though." He turned and waved to the others, beckoning them on.

It was a relief to be heading downwards. Sand spilled from every heavy footstep, cascading down the sides of the valley. Jade and the others built up a momentum that carried them quickly down the steep bank.

Soon they were close enough to see what the dark shape at the bottom was.

"I'm guessing that isn't a good sign," Rich gasped.

It was a dead camel.

"Depends how long it's been dead," said Chance. He skidded to a halt at the bottom of the sand dune, close to the corpse.

"A while, I'd say," said Chuck, arriving beside Chance, Rich and Jade.

Kate Hunter was just behind him. "I'm not eating that," she said.

Jade was doing her best not to be sick from the smell. Kate's words almost tipped her over the edge. "Gross," she gasped.

"We may not have a lot of choice," said Chance. He waved his hand to try to get rid of some of the flies that had left the dead camel to investigate the newcomers. "Doubt there's any blood left to drink, and you're right, the meat will be rancid. What's left of it."

"You're doing this deliberately," said Jade, turning away.

She didn't need to look any closer at the camel to know it had been dead for days. The carcass was covered in flies, the flesh and skin stripped away in places.

"Well, at least we know we're not far from a pathway or route of some kind," said Chance.

"One dead camel tells you that?" said Rich. "It could have just wandered here and got lost. It is dead, after all."

"I assume there are wild camels," said Kate. "He's right; it probably just got lost or wandered off sick or something."

"You can see where it was wearing a bridle," said Chuck quietly. "John's right. This animal belonged to someone. Out in the desert, you don't lose a camel, not unless you're really unlucky."

"So, there might be people around?" asked Jade. Suddenly things didn't seem quite so bad. "Maybe we can find them. Can we signal or something?"

"You're assuming that they'll be friendly," Chuck told her.

"Won't they?" said Rich.

"They might resent us being in their territory," said Chance. "Or they might be rebel fighters who'll happily kill any foreigners they find – especially Americans and Britions. At best they'll just resent having to provide more people with food and water and leave us here."

"Glad I asked," muttered Rich.

"And the good news is?" Jade prompted. Despite the smell and the grossness of it all, she couldn't help looking at the poor, dead animal. She was trying to see the bridle Chuck had spotted, but the whole thing was just a desiccated mess of hair and bone and…

"The good news is that we can't be far from a recognised route. And a route has to go somewhere," Chance was saying.

But Jade was no longer listening. She was staring at the rotting carcass, unable to believe what she was seeing. "It's moving," she said. "Look – there, in its side, there's something moving."

The hole in the camel's side was a dark blotch of shadow. But part of that darkness was detaching itself, clawing its way out of the side of the camel. Pale legs reached out, gripping the side of the wound. A massive, bulbous shape heaved itself out of the dead camel.

"Oh – my – God," said Rich.

Kate Hunter gave a shriek of horror.

Chuck and Chance backed slowly away.

The spider that crawled down the side of the camel was the size of a plate – easily fifteen centimetres across. The pale legs were attached to a long, dark, segmented body. The head was fiery red, like the head of an ant, but stubbled with coarse hair and ending with a vicious double set of pincers. The creature paused on the matted hairy hide, legs quivering and dark body pulsing slightly.

Then another one climbed out after it, and scuttled across the camel's body before dropping to the sand just metres away from Jade and the others.

"Remind me," said Chuck quietly, "do we stand absolutely still, or do we run like hell?"

"Who are you asking?" replied Rich. "And what makes you think any of us know?"

"John?" Chuck asked Chance.

"Not a clue."

"Reckon we should run then," said Kate, still backing slowly away. "I mean, how fast can a spider go?"

Kate had scarcely finished speaking when the nearest spider jumped. Its whole body tensed, then the legs snapped out and the creature was flying towards Jade.

Even though she was two metres away, the spider hurtled straight at her. Jade gave a shriek and lashed out. Her hand connected with the spider, knocking it sideways. The pale-bodied creature crashed down at Jade's feet. It was almost as big as her shoe – bigger than the hand she had thumped it with.

Jade didn't wait, just turned and ran, her feet sticking and sliding in the sand. The spider was following her, tracking Jade's shadow across the valley, keeping up with her.

Behind Jade, the others were running too. The second spider was a dark shape gaining on Chuck and Kate. Rich and Chance were climbing up the steep valley side.

Jade dodged suddenly sideways, but the spider changed direction too. It wasn't gaining on her, but it was keeping pace. She glanced down, saw the pincers working, and ran faster. The spider stayed with her. It was playing with her – it could catch her whenever it wanted.

So Jade stopped, and kicked out. The spider darted aside, and she missed. Then it came at her again. Another leap and Jade barely ducked out of the way in time. She could see Kate and Chuck were climbing the bank. Maybe the spider couldn't cope with the slope. Jade staggered up the steep incline. Each step she took, she slipped back down with cascades of sand. She kicked at the valley wall, sending an avalanche down over the spider – burying it.

But moments later, sharp pincers emerged from the sand as the creature burrowed out and came after her again.

Jade reached the top, too exhausted to go on. Her legs buckled under her and she slumped to the ground. Her cheek was pressed to the burning sand. The spider was scuttling rapidly towards her, pincers clicking hungrily.

It halted just centimetres away, head swaying slightly as if watching her. At the same moment, a shadow fell across Jade. The heat and glare of the sun were blotted out by a figure.

All around, along the top of the sand dune, dozens of figures were rising up. Their robes were tattered and faded, their dark faces weathered by years in the desert.

The man standing over Jade raised a rifle, holding it in one hand. The spider quivered in anticipation and the man let out an angry roar, then brought the gun slamming down towards Jade's head.

14

There was a sickening crunch as the spider was crushed beneath the butt of the gun. The man reached down with his other hand and helped Jade to her feet.

He barely spared her a glance. The man was looking over her shoulder, and his face split into a massive grin.

"English!" he exclaimed.

Jade watched in amazement as the man stepped forward and dragged her dad into an enormous hug.

"We meet again, English," the man said, shaking with laughter. "It has been a long time, but now you have come for your camel, no?"

Picking up on his cue, the other figures also began to laugh. Soon the desert echoed with the sound of their mirth.

"You speak their language?" asked Chuck.

Chance shrugged. "Enough to get by. Kassim's English is good enough for us to understand each other."

"And you really have a camel?" asked Rich.

"Well, sort of. I did these guys a favour a while back. They gave me a camel as a thank you and I said they could look after it for me till I came back." He frowned. "I just hope they don't expect me to take it with me when we go."

Jade was sipping from a small leather bag filled with water. "Our own camel could be useful."

Kassim arrived in time to hear this, and he laughed again. "Only you English would be brave enough to come into the desert without water or a camel."

"Americans—" Kate started to say, but Chance gestured to her to be quiet.

"Americans?" Kassim spat on his hand. "Only Americans would be *foolish* enough." He glared suspiciously at Kate. "Are you brave or foolish?"

"Brave," she said quickly. "Always brave."

"Except when there are spiders about," said Chuck quietly.

But Kassim heard him. "Camel spiders are no danger."

"Camel spiders?" said Jade. "Is that what they were?"

"Some call them desert spiders, or wind scorpions. They usually hunt at night. Insects, birds – even real scorpions are their prey. They crush scorpions so fast they cannot sting."

Jade grimaced, but Kassim laughed again.

"They do not attack us. Not usually, not unless they are frightened. They have no poison, but they can bite. Very nasty bite."

"So why was that one chasing me?" Jade demanded.

Kassim rattled off an explanation in his own language, then shrugged apologetically.

"I think he said they lie in wait for insects and birds close to dead camels. The reason they were chasing us is that they like the shade," Chance explained. "That spider wasn't actually interested in you, Jade. He just wanted to stay cool. He was chasing your shadow."

"And you killed it?" Jade accused.

Kassim's eyes widened in surprise. "Next one we find, I catch it for you as a pet," he said. Then he turned to Chance. "Now, since we are speaking of pets, I have your camel still. You can have him if you wish, or I can make a trade with you."

"You want to buy my camel back?" said Chance, amused.

"I think a deal would suit us both. We are very civilised people now. We speak English, we have modern equipment." Kassim gave another gap-toothed grin. "You give me back the camel, and I will let you use our radio. Deal?"

Chance didn't need to check with the others. He nodded. "Deal."

The expert at the British Museum was called Julius and he was younger than Jade had expected. For some reason she'd thought that someone who knew all about ancient artefacts and antiquities would be old. In fact, he looked about the same age as her dad.

The journey back had been swift. Ardman might not have been able to arrange another helicopter to get them out of the desert quickly, but Chuck's colleagues in Washington had. Jade and her brother and father had said goodbye to Chuck and Kate when they reached Kuwait. It was a parting tinged with sadness as they remembered the Americans' colleagues who would not return. But Jade was also happy and relieved to be safe and well and back with her family. She and Rich slept for most of the flight back to Heathrow – which was just as well, since a car was waiting at the arrivals terminal to whisk them straight to the British Museum.

Now they were in a small, book-lined office in the Department of Antiquities. The pictures from Chance's mobile phone had been printed out and computer-enhanced. They were spread out on the old mahogany desk that dominated the small room. Julius was examining one of them through an eyeglass. He straightened up, the eyeglass dropping into his waiting hand.

"Any ideas?" asked Chance.

"A few. None of them very useful, I'm afraid." Julius tapped the photo he had been examining. "The design suggests it's old. Maybe even Babylonian."

"Valuable?" asked Rich eagerly.

"Oh yes. But not outrageously. If it's genuine and not a later copy, then we're talking thousands, not tens of thousands of pounds."

"The people who wanted it went to a lot of trouble

for something that's only worth thousands of pounds," said Chance.

"Maybe it's more valuable to them. Some symbolic or personal value."

"Or it's not quite what it seems."

Julius smiled. "Nothing is ever *quite* what it seems."

"Could it be much older than you think?" asked Jade. "Would that make it more valuable?"

"It would," Julius conceded. "But without the actual statue there's no way of knowing. Its provenance might be important, but that would be hard to prove."

"What do you mean?" asked Rich.

"Well, if this statue was once owned by – or even made for – Alexander the Great, then it would be worth a lot more to a collector or a museum than if it was just one of a dozen that was owned by Joe Smith. But, as I say, proving that was the case would be tricky. You'd need some accompanying documentation, or an unambiguous reference to this specific piece in some account from the period."

"Maybe that's what Darrow has," said Jade. "Maybe that's why he's suddenly interested in the statue again after all this time, because he's found some document that proves it's worth millions."

"It's a nice looking piece," Julius admitted. "Can I ask why you left it in the desert in the first place?"

"Too heavy to carry, simple as that."

"Really?" Julius frowned and leafed through the pictures again. "How heavy?"

Chance shrugged. "Five kilos. Give or take."

"It shouldn't weigh anything like that much." He tapped his chin with a thoughtful finger. "It was definitely ceramic rather than stone?"

"Terracotta, something like that."

"I've got a bit of it here, if that helps," said Rich.

Julius looked up from the pictures. "It certainly does."

Rich took the beetle clicker toy from his pocket. He turned it upside down and levered up the strip of metal that made the clicking noise. Then he tipped out the sliver of material Chance had chipped off the base of the statue.

Julius examined it through his eyeglass. "Ceramic of some sort. Pottery…" He sat back in his chair. "I'll get some tests done and let you know if we find out anything useful. But on the face of it, I have to say, it's an interesting, but unremarkable piece."

Ardman convened a meeting in the library of Algernon's house. The only other people present were Jade, Rich and Chance. Alan and Pete had tracked Darrow and the helicopters for at least some of their journey.

"They have a short range capacity, so there's not many places they could have come from or gone to," explained Pete.

"Well, only one, realistically," added Alan. "We'd know if they went to Kuwait. And Iran's pretty well covered, so it's unlikely they got in and out without us seeing them."

"Could they be local to Iraq?" asked Ardman.

Pete shook his head. "Got the possible locations in that country under so much air surveillance we'd know if a pigeon took off or landed."

"Which, given the range and the direction we last had them heading, leaves East Araby," Alan told them.

"I thought that was a friendly country," said Jade, remembering their discussions in the desert.

"It is," said Chance. "But no one said this was any sort of official or sanctioned mission. Darrow obviously has influence, and probably money."

"So why's he need the statue?" asked Rich.

"Why indeed?" echoed Ardman. "Whatever is going on, we can't afford to upset King Hassan, or allow Darrow to do anything that might sour our relations with East Araby. Especially now the elections are coming up."

"The helicopters were military," said Chance. "Maybe things have already gone sour. Maybe Hassan is working against us."

"Unlikely," said Ardman. "He's always been very pro-US and -UK, but there are factions within the military who don't take kindly to American nuclear weapons and Stealth Bombers being based in their country." He turned to Alan. "Have you got a picture of Hassan?"

"There'll be one on the web. Give us a second."

Moments later, Alan swung one of the monitors round so they could all see the photograph it displayed. A man's face – dark, handsome, with a neatly trimmed black beard and deep-set eyes. The man was smiling; a kindly face.

A face that Jade recognised.

"That's King Hassan?"

"Sure is," said Alan. "Official portrait."

Jade was shaking her head in disbelief. "But that's

the man at the desert villa, the man who held me captive."

"You're sure?" asked Ardman.

Jade nodded. "He said something about his people. About how I was doing his country a great service."

Ardman was frowning. "It sounds like we may have misjudged the situation rather badly."

"Jade," said Chance, "you're absolutely sure that this is the man?"

"I'm sure." There was no doubt in her mind. "I mean, it's obviously an old photo, because his beard's gone grey and he's much older now than he is there." She pointed at the screen.

Ardman's frown deepened. "When was that portrait taken?"

Alan checked something on another screen. "The press release says it was taken in May."

"What year?" asked Ardman impatiently.

"This year."

Ardman nodded as if he had expected this. "That photo certainly looks like the King Hassan that *I* remember. He's a relatively young man." He turned to Jade. "Perhaps you met someone else – someone who looks like King Hassan, but older. Did he give you any clue as to who he might be?"

"He said his name was Ali. I assumed that was just a pseudonym."

"Or maybe not." Ardman went over to the keyboard Alan had been using and typed something in. A few seconds and several mouse clicks later, the picture changed to what looked like an older version of the same man.

"That's him!" said Jade. "Without a doubt. That's exactly what he looked like."

Ardman nodded grimly. "That is Crown Prince Ali, the King's uncle. Until the King was born, he was heir to the throne. And he is heir to the throne still, until the King has a son."

"A throne that will have no power after the elections," said Chance. "His nephew is in effect abdicating, and staying on only as a figurehead in the new democracy."

"Ali is fiercely opposed to the democratisation of his country," Ardman agreed. "He feels he was cheated of the throne nearly thirty years ago when his brother's wife turned out to be expecting a child after King Omar died. Ali reckoned he had the top job, and then he lost out to a baby. He's tried to influence the child ever since, but had to watch as the country's moved closer to the West, and the US installed bases in return for aid and funding that Ali doesn't want."

"So he's just a powerless would-be dictator?" said Rich.

"Not quite powerless," said Chance. "He's head of the country's armed forces. So he certainly has access to helicopter gunships."

"He also has a private palace right slap bang in the middle of the Araby Desert," Pete announced. "I've got some nice satellite images here. Private helipad, rooftop pool, and golden sand as far as the eye can see in every direction, except for a small private airstrip."

"Sounds familiar," said Jade. "And like I told you, there's a secret laboratory too."

Chance's mobile rang, and he glanced at the display before answering it. The conversation was short, Chance murmuring a thank you and ending the call.

"That was Julius," he said, "and it sounds like the answers can't come soon enough. He's analysed the pottery shard we gave him, and he managed to estimate the age of the statue."

"It's ancient, isn't it?" said Rich. "Got to be. Worth millions, I bet."

"Not exactly," said Chance. "Julius says he can't give an exact date, but all the tests suggest that the statue was made less than thirty years ago."

15

With evidence from John Chance as well as Chuck and his American colleagues, Ardman had little trouble getting authorisation for the raid on the desert palace where Jade had been held. Its isolation – an advantage to Crown Prince Ali when plotting against his nephew – had now become its greatest weakness. Hidden away from view, Ardman's team could get away with the sort of operation they'd never be permitted to stage if there was any risk of witnesses.

Ardman had rather more trouble persuading Jade and Rich that they were not going.

"I was there," Jade pointed out. "I know the layout, I can show you where their underground lab is hidden."

"You only found an observation gallery," said Ardman. "There must be another way in."

"Not that's shown on the builders' plans," said Alan. "I've got a schematic here, and there's no reference to a secret underground laboratory."

"Not that we really thought there would be," Pete added quickly. "I mean, that's what *secret* means, right?"

"I'm going," said Jade. "That's final. These guys kept me prisoner. It's payback time and I'm going to be there paying back."

Ardman sighed, sensing defeat.

"And I'm going too," said Rich. "If Jade's going, so am I."

"Right," said Jade.

"She needs looking after," Rich went on.

"Wrong!" Jade snapped.

"Really? Look what happened last time."

"Excuse me." Jade put her hands on her hips and stared him down. "I was the one who *didn't* get caught by the people we were trying to escape from. Even if they did turn out to be the good guys. Who needs help?"

"Children," said Chance firmly.

"Oh, come on, Dad," insisted Rich. "Jade's right. She needs to be there and I'm coming too."

Chance looked from one to the other. "It's up to Ardman," he said. "But if he agrees you can come, and I'll admit it will be useful to have Jade along, then you both stay in the helicopter until and unless I tell you otherwise."

Jade hugged him. "Thanks, Dad."

"Check with Ardman," said Chance again.

Jade untangled herself and turned to face her dad's superior. "Well?"

Ardman sucked in his cheeks as he considered. Finally, he said: "It's your show, John. And they're your children."

Chance nodded. "Tell me about it."

There were three helicopters in the attack. The first two carried the assault teams – the third held back. Inside were Rich and Jade, along with two scientists from the Ministry of Defence whose job it was to work out what the laboratory was for.

The third helicopter was less advanced than the others, and less well armoured. The front of the cabin was in effect a wide window, so Rich and Jade had a good view of what was happening.

The lead helicopters were so advanced they weren't officially in service yet. Nicknamed 'Future Lynx' they were updated versions of the Westland Lynx, which had been in service with the British armed forces since the 1970s. These new variants were not officially due to be delivered to the MOD until 2011, and wouldn't see active service until 2014. But 'officially' was different from reality.

For Ardman's mission, they were ideal. Since the advanced prototypes did not officially exist, no one could trace them back to the British. And for the development team working with the AgustaWestland company, the chance of a real battlefield test mission was too good to miss.

Another advantage was that the Lynx was the fastest helicopter in the world, and the new variants were even quicker than the originals. They screamed across the desert, accelerating to over 300 kilometres an hour as they approached their target, leaving Rich and Jade's helicopter far behind.

The disadvantage was they only had room inside for three people. This was why the SAS team was braced to the helicopters' specially reinforced skids.

As the aircraft neared their target, they slowed. The dark-clad SAS men dropped on ropes so that they were hanging beneath the Lynxes – four from each helicopter.

Missiles ripped out from the two helicopters. Precisely targeted, they tore into the side of the palace. Windows exploded in fragments of glass. Two of the SAS men on each helicopter dropped further on their ropes. As the helicopters powered over the palace, they let go and were hurled in through the gaping holes left by the missiles.

Above the palace, the Lynxes slowed again, allowing the other four men to drop to the roof. Then the helicopters sped up to take position well out of range of any counter measures or gunfire. They hovered behind the palace like deadly dark insects in the startlingly blue sky.

The windows of the palace were lit orange as the assault team checked each room. Any resistance and a stun grenade soon stopped it.

Through their headsets, Rich and Jade could hear the terse communication between the soldiers.

"Area three – clear."

"Roof area – four down. Now clear."

"Area five – clear. Three down."

Smoke was rising from the holes in the front of the palace. A dark cloud staining the azure sky.

"Kitchens – secure. Staff contained."

Finally, they heard their dad's satisfied tone: "All areas secure. Objective secured."

The scientist sitting behind Rich looked more like a police forensics officer in his white coverall. He leaned forward as he spoke into a microphone.

"Have you found the lab?"

"Affirmative," Chance's voice came back through the headphones. "No sign of scientists or staff. Place looks abandoned, but we haven't gone inside, we'll wait for you."

The scientist nodded to his colleague. "On our way." He gave the helicopter pilot a thumbs-up, and the aircraft dipped its nose and powered forwards.

Chance was waiting for them on the rooftop helicopter pad, a machinegun slung over his shoulder.

"Looks like you stayed in a good hotel," Rich told Jade as they made their way past the pool. The scientists followed them, each carrying a large metal briefcase of equipment.

A black-clad soldier was dragging an unconscious gunman from the water as they passed.

"Thirsty work, sir," he said to Chance as he heaved the man on to the side and removed his gun from the holster. The guard hadn't even had time to draw it as the SAS stormed in.

"This is a dry country," Chance told him.

"You should tell this guy."

Rich was surprised how much cooler it became as soon as they were inside. Smoke drifted through the palace. There was dust and debris everywhere from the SAS attack. They passed several unhappy looking men in combat gear handcuffed to banisters or heavy furniture. Others lay face down in rooms reduced to rubble. Rich didn't look too closely.

Chance led Rich, Jade and the two scientists down a wide stone staircase to an entrance hall. From here they went along a wide passageway to a metal door. There was a charred hole in the door where the lock had been blown out.

"This is as far as we got," Chance told the scientists. "It's up to you now."

He pushed open the door and gestured for them to go inside. Rich saw that both the men had pulled on breathing masks attached to small oxygen cylinders on their backs.

"Not taking any chances, then," he said to Jade.

Through the door was a small entrance lobby that ended at another door, this one made of glass. Beyond that was a second glass door – an airlock.

"Sterile atmosphere," said one of the scientists, his voice filtered and distorted by the mask.

Rich, Jade and Chance watched the scientists make their way through the two glass doors.

"It looks abandoned," said Jade. "When I was here a couple of days ago, there were people working. It was very busy."

"They couldn't have known we were coming," said Chance. "So we have to assume they finished whatever they were doing."

One of the scientists was checking a device strapped to his wrist. He showed it to his colleague, and they both nodded. Then the first scientist pulled off his mask. Rich could see him sniffing the air hesitantly.

"Looks OK," said Chance. "But you two stay here until we're absolutely sure."

The outer airlock door opened with a slight hiss, and Chance went through. As soon as the door was sealed behind him, he pressed the button to open the inner door. There was a pause while the filters checked the air between the two doors for contamination.

Just as the inner door started to open, there was movement from deeper inside the lab. A dark figure was silhouetted against the pale wall as he stood up, raising a machine gun.

One of the scientists saw the gunman, and pushed the other to one side, before diving to the floor.

The inner door was swinging slowly open. The gunman opened fire – not at the scientists, but at Chance.

The front of the airlock door crazed over in a mass of cracks as the bullets impacted. Before the gunman could fire again, Chance was gone – through the half-open door, and rolling across the floor. He sprang to his feet metres away from where the gunman was aiming. A single controlled burst of gunfire slammed the gunman back into the wall.

Rich and Jade both ran for the airlock as fast as they could. The inner door had jammed half open, the mechanism damaged by the gunfire.

The scientists were getting to their feet as Rich and Jade arrived. But Rich was looking at the body of the gunman Chance had just shot. One of the man's eyebrows ended above the eye, a pale scar curling down his left cheek.

"The gunman from the farm," said Jade. "He was with Darrow at *Boscombe Heights* too."

"As we suspected, it was a set-up," said Chance, joining them. "McCain wanted it to look like he was in real trouble, so I'd help him. Even before he found out I wasn't there, they'd agreed to stage a pursuit. Then he carried on with it to convince you he was in trouble so you'd get me involved and help him. It must have surprised him a bit when Chuck White's team joined in as well."

As they moved through the lab, examining each workbench and set of apparatus in turn, the scientists gradually became quieter and more serious.

Rich knew not to touch anything, but before long he was getting bored. Jade and Chance were talking quietly at one end of the large laboratory. She pointed up at a huge window overlooking the room, and Rich guessed that was where she had seen it from originally.

He turned to walk back and join them. There was nothing here that made much sense to him. OK, he recognised laptop computers and a large shredder. He could understand the containment chamber with its rubber sleeves and gloves extending inside the sealed glass case. There were even Bunsen burners and racks of test tubes like in the school science lab. But Rich had no idea what it was all for.

As he turned, his foot caught on something sticking out from under the workbench. It gave a metallic clang, and he held his hands up in apology as one of the scientists turned to glare at him.

Rich looked to see what he'd kicked. It was a metal waste bin. It was strange seeing something so ordinary in the hi-tech environment. He nudged it back under the workbench with his foot and turned to go.

Then his brain registered what he had seen inside, and he knelt down to grab the bin and pull it back out into the light.

"Over here!" called Rich. "I think you should see this."

He lifted the bin up on to the workbench, careful not to disturb the fragments inside.

"What is it?" asked Chance, joining him. The two scientists and Jade were close behind.

"It's just fragments, something broken," one of the scientists said. "Junk. Rubbish."

Rich shook his head. "It's pottery. Ceramic. I think it's the remains of the statue."

Dad picked up the bin and upended it, spilling the contents across the workbench. Most of the pieces of dull, brown ceramic were too small to be recognisable. But a large part of a weathered lion's head stared back up at them from the workbench.

"Why did they break it?" Jade wondered. She picked up the piece of the head and turned it over, examining it. "Was it an accident, do you think?" She frowned. "It's not as heavy as I expected, after what you said."

One of the scientists was gently teasing several pieces of the shattered statue together like a three-dimensional jigsaw.

The other pointed to where several pieces joined. "Impact damage. Maybe a hammer."

"They *deliberately* broke it?" said Rich.

"We're looking for something about this big," said the first scientist. He held his hands slightly apart. "Probably made of metal. And…" he glanced at his colleague, who mirrored his grim expression. "And probably lead-lined."

"There's a thing looks like a small thermos flask

over there," said Jade, pointing to one of the other workbenches.

One of the scientists hurried over, collecting his metal case of equipment on the way.

"What is it?" asked Chance.

"I need to know exactly where this statue came from," said the scientist.

"Wish we knew," Rich told him. "We thought it was ancient, but it turns out it was made only recently."

The scientist held some of the broken pieces together. "See this smooth area inside? The statue was cast round something else."

"There was something inside it?" said Jade.

"Makes sense," agreed Chance. "Something hidden. Something heavy."

The scientist was nodding. "And we need to know where it came from." He turned and spread his hands. "This whole place, it's been cleared out. But there's enough here to know what it was for."

"Which was?" said Rich.

"It's a small nuclear facility. Oh, I don't mean a reactor or anything," he said, catching sight of Rich's expression. "I mean it's for processing small amounts of nuclear material."

"But nuclear material is very hard to get hold of, isn't it?" said Jade. "That's what all the fuss is with Iran and North Korea and places like that, because they're trying to make it."

"Is that what they were doing here?" asked Rich. "Processing plutonium or something?"

"No," said the scientist. "I'm afraid this is the other end of the process."

From across the room came an angry clicking sound. The other scientist had opened the metal container Jade had seen, and was holding a device over the open top. He closed the canister up again quickly. He looked pale.

"I'm guessing it's not cold coffee, then," said Jade quietly.

"This lab," the first scientist told them, "is for putting together the components of a small nuclear device."

"Device? You mean – a *bomb*?" Rich gasped.

"I mean a bomb. And for that they needed weapons-grade nuclear material."

"But where would they get it?" said Jade.

It was Chacewho answered. "From a secret Iraqi nuclear installation that was destroyed before the first

Gulf War. It was smuggled out by Darrow, hidden inside what looked like an antique statue of a lion. That's what he's really been after all this time. Maybe he was in the pay of Saddam Hussein and smuggling out his precious plutonium when we blew up the plant. They obviously had it all ready for him to take. He must have been rather miffed when we left it behind in the desert."

"But now he's got it back," said Rich. "Now Crown Prince Ali has a nuclear bomb."

Chance nodded. "And we have no idea where it is, or what he plans to do with it."

16

The discovery at the lab changed everything. Suddenly Ardman's team was officially welcomed. King Hassan was informed of their arrival and the situation, but spared some of the details of the attack on his uncle's desert palace. That same desert palace was now turned into the nerve centre of the operation to search for the missing nuclear device.

"There's no sign of Crown Prince Ali," Ardman explained at a hurried update briefing as soon as he arrived at the palace.

They were all gathered in what had been an enormous dining room. One of Ardman's senior staff, a man called Goddard, was now in charge of clearing up the mess Chance's team had made and of sifting through the debris and searching the palace for any clues as to where the bomb had been taken.

Pete and Alan had set up their equipment in another reception room, while there seemed to be a never-ending stream of helicopters arriving and leaving from the roof and small jets from the airstrip a quarter of a mile away.

Rich and Jade were sitting at the back of the briefing. Chance was at the front of the room, together with Dex and a few other men in military uniforms. One of the two scientists was also there, the other still working in the laboratory to piece together exactly what had happened there.

"King Hassan can't just denounce his uncle," Ardman was explaining. "He's got people he can trust looking for him, but Ali has a lot of support in the military. He could be on any number of army bases or airfields."

"With his bomb," Chance added.

"Indeed. Now, we have put out pictures of Darrow. Every police station, army base or citizen who watches TV knows he's a dangerous criminal and with luck someone will have seen him. That may give us some leads."

224

"If he hasn't already scarpered," said Goddard from the doorway. He was just back from checking on how his team was doing. "I mean, he's delivered the statue – so he's probably taken his dosh and done a runner."

Chance shook his head. "I think after the trouble we've given him – and he must know by now what's happened here – Darrow will want to be in at the kill." He turned to Halford. "What do you think?"

"I think that's right," Dex agreed. "He's not one to walk away from something before it's finished. That said, he'll want to make sure he's well away from the place the bomb's going to go off."

"If it is," muttered Rich.

Ardman heard him. "I'm sorry – what was that?"

Rich looked down at his feet, embarrassed.

"No," Ardman went on, "I want to know. I'm not telling you off for talking in class. We're in a bit of a fix, to say the least, so if you have a comment I really do want to hear it, Rich."

Rich looked up. "I was just wondering if they intend to set off the bomb at all. The threat might be enough for whatever they're after."

"That's right," said Jade. "I mean, they can only set it off once. After that, the threat is gone."

"It *is* a nuclear bomb," Ardman pointed out.

The scientist stood up, ready to make a point. "True, but from the amount of material we believe they have, it's relatively small. It could take out a suburb of the capital city, and it would cause lots of collateral damage from the radiation and electromagnetic pulse, but in nuclear terms, she's a midget. Maybe the threat is greater than the reality." He shrugged apologetically, and sat down again.

"No," said Chance. "I don't know about Crown Prince Ali, but if Darrow has in effect provided a weapon – any weapon – he'll want to see it used."

There was silence for several moments, then Ardman snapped, "Suggestions?"

"What's Ali's end game? What's he really want to achieve from all this?" asked Dex. "If we knew that, we could take a stab at how he plans to achieve it."

"I think we can assume he wants to stop the elections," said Ardman. "Ideally, his dream scenario if you like, would be to seize absolute power from his nephew and chuck out the Americans."

In the doorway, Goddard was talking quietly into a radio. He raised his hand as he finished the conversation.

"Yes, Mr Goddard?" Ardman prompted.

"That was Pete. He thinks they might be on to something. There's a couple of laptop computers down in the lab. Not much of any use on them, but Alan's working on the hard discs to see what's been erased."

"And what's Pete doing?" asked Chance.

"He's found a shredder."

Rich recalled seeing the shredder in the lab. "How does that help?" he asked.

"After the Iranians took the US Embassy there, they got students to go through the shredded documents and piece them back together like a jigsaw," said Ardman. "But it took years. Please tell me Pete has a rather more timely solution to the problem."

Goddard shrugged. "Well, sir, you never know."

Jade nudged Rich. "Come on, let's go and see if we can help. This is boring and we're not going to learn anything new."

"Where are we going?" Rich asked as he followed Jade out.

"You heard Ardman. The Iranians got students to put the shredded documents back together."

"So?"

"So, we're students, aren't we?" said Jade.

They made their way back down to the laboratory.

"Ardman said it took them years, though," said Rich. "How long have you got?"

In the lab, Alan was hard at work at one of the computers that had been left behind. He glanced up as Jade and Rich came in.

"Good job they didn't know we were coming," he said. "Or they'd have taken these with them, or destroyed them completely. Same goes for the remains of that statue and the containment flask. Then we'd have no idea what they're up to."

"You found anything useful so far?" asked Rich.

Alan shook his head. "Lots of technical stuff about the weapon. Bomb design and emails between Ali and Darrow. Incriminating, but not very helpful." He settled back into his work.

Pete had tipped the contents of the shredder out on to the next workbench. He was gently teasing apart the mound of thin strips of paper.

"Looks like fun," said Jade.

"Yeah, terrific. Luckily the shredder doesn't cross cut as well, so we have all these long strips like fettuccini pasta."

"Can we help?" asked Rich.

"If you can get the strips separated and intact, then I can scan them in. Once I've got images of each shredded strip in the computer, I've written a program that will try to match them up."

"Will it take long?" asked Jade.

"Probably. The real problem is that there are so many different sheets, some of them double-sided. The program just tries each strip against every other until it finds two that fit together. If we could cut down the number of possible combinations it would be a lot quicker."

Rich and Jade set to work at opposite sides of the pile of shredded paper. It was slow, meticulous work to take a strip of paper carefully from the pile without tearing it. Sometimes, several strands were close together, looped through the others in the same way. They tried to keep these together, as it seemed likely they were from the same sheet – or the same few sheets fed through the shredder at the same time.

Pete took the separated shreds of paper over to a small desktop scanner. This was attached to a computer. Rich could see images of each strand appearing on the screen. The program slowly worked through different combinations, as it tried to match the shape of the torn edges and the printed words. It was obviously going to take a very long time.

"It's a shame some of the sheets weren't a different colour," Jade complained as she eased another strand of paper from the pile and smoothed it out. "If they'd colour-coded their plans, like using yellow paper for anything really useful and important and blue for stuff that doesn't matter, then that would speed things up, wouldn't it?"

"Certainly would," agreed Pete.

"Or if they'd just shredded less stuff," Rich muttered. He prised apart some of the tightly packed paper as he followed the piece he was trying to get out. It was easy to keep track of the strip of paper he wanted if he angled his head slightly because it caught and reflected the light.

With the shredded strip finally free, Rich smoothed it out and put it on the end of the workbench ready for Pete to scan.

He was halfway through recovering another strip when he realised what he had done.

"Hang on!" he said out loud, hurrying back to the separated strips of paper arranged at the end of the workbench.

Jade and Pete both heard something in his tone of voice and hurried over. Alan glanced up from his work.

"What is it?" said Jade.

"What you said about different coloured paper." Rich picked up the strip he had just put down with the others. "It was easy to see this strip, because it caught the light. Look – it's glossy. The rest is just ordinary printer paper, but this is from a sheet that's different."

"Let me see." Pete took the paper carefully from Rich. "You're right. This is a coated paper from an inkjet printer. Not that we have any idea if that means it's more or less important, but at least we can deal with the glossy paper separately from the rest. Should speed things up a lot."

They separated the sorted strips into two piles. There were already several glossy shreds of paper, and because it was easy to spot now they'd thought of it, Rich and Jade concentrated on finding more. There were not that many, and most of them were close together – suggesting they came from a single set of pages.

Pete scanned in the glossy strips first. The computer was soon assembling them rapidly into just one single large sheet on the computer screen.

"Looks like a map or a plan," said Jade. Buildings, roads… Wonder where it is."

"I'll get Dad," said Rich. "Maybe he'll have some idea of where this is and if it's important."

It was important, and it was frightening. As soon as he saw it, Chance recognised the plan as a map of a military installation. Comparing the plan with satellite images, it didn't take long for Pete to find a match. Within the hour, most of the team were leaving the desert palace and heading for the main American airbase in East Araby.

"Why not just tell the Americans and start a full-scale search?" Jade yelled to Chance over the sound of the helicopter engines.

"And start a panic as well? There are families based there, and it's on the outskirts of the capital."

"Then evacuate everyone," said Rich.

Chance shook his head. "Can't afford for King Hassan to look like he's losing control. Any hint of trouble, and the hardliners he's fought to get on board will insist he postpone the elections. They'd never restage them."

"So that's why Ali has planted the bomb on the US base?" asked Jade. "Just to frighten his brother out of the elections?"

"No, it's not that simple." Chance leaned towards his children. "He's going to set off the bomb, no question."

"But why?" Rich wondered.

"Think about it. A nuclear explosion on a US airbase where they station Stealth Bombers. What will everyone think happened? They won't believe that Crown Prince Ali got access to nuclear technology and blew up part of his own capital city."

Jade could see what he was getting at. "Everyone will think there was an accident. They'll think it was an American nuke that went off by accident."

"And then?" Chance prompted.

"The elections will be called off because of the crisis," said Rich, "and King Hassan will have to throw out the Americans."

"That's only two out of three of Ali's goals," said Jade.

"The third comes easily enough. After the blast, Ali will insist on imposing martial law. And he's head of the armed forces. Hassan may cling to power for a while, but he'll be finished. He invited the Americans in, remember. Then he showed weakness by planning the elections. The generals who aren't already on Ali's side will soon come over to him. It'll be a coup in all but name."

"And thousands of people will die," said Jade.

"Tens of thousands. Unless we find the bomb before it goes off."

"No pressure then," said Jade.

Rich nodded. "Let's just hope it doesn't go off while we're there looking for it."

"I guess the situation couldn't be much worse," agreed Jade.

"That's why you're not staying," Dad told her.

Jade didn't answer. She looked at Rich, and he nodded slightly. This was a discussion they could save for later.

Their helicopter was coming in to land at the edge of one of the runways on the airbase. Huge transport planes were lined up off to one side. The angular nose of a B-2 Stealth Bomber was poking out of a nearby hanger. A Jeep bumped rapidly over the grass towards the helicopter as it touched down.

Inside the Jeep, Jade was surprised to see Chuck

White and Kate Hunter, back in their business suits despite the heat, and wearing their dark glasses.

"Looks like they're on duty," she said. She meant it as a joke.

But Chance didn't look like he was joking. "Then the situation just got a whole lot worse," he said.

"We've organised a search of the base," said Chuck White, as soon as they were in a private briefing room in the main admin block.

"As few people as possible know what's really going on," Kate Hunter explained. "But we're on a tight schedule. We can't afford to delay or change what's going on."

"How long do we have?" asked Chance.

"Nine hours," said Chuck.

"Nine hours till the bomb goes off?" said Jade. "How do you know?"

"We don't," Kate told her. "But nine hours is how long we have to find it and neutralise the threat. Otherwise…" She blew out a long breath.

"I have a team of agents coordinating things from here," Chuck went on. "The best thing you guys can do is probably get the hell out of here."

"Can't we help?" said Rich. "We want to stop this as much as you do."

"It's our job now," Kate told him.

"Darrow is British," said Jade, "and the threat is to the people of East Araby, even if this is a US base. You could evacuate everyone."

"Not an option," said Chuck. "Like Kate told you, we're on a tight schedule. Any change now, and Crown Prince Ali's propaganda guys will have a field day. They'll say that the King is in an untenable position, and the US President is a weak-minded coward."

"What's the President got to do with this?" asked Rich, confused. "He's safe and sound in Washington, isn't he? I mean, he agrees the funding and aid I suppose, but…" His voice tailed off as he remembered something that Dex had told him when they first met Chuck.

"What is it?" said Jade.

Rich was looking straight at Chuck. "You're not anything to do with the CIA, are you? Dex told us that. Dad too."

"That's right," said Chuck quietly.

"So what?" said Jade. "They're National Security or whatever. What difference does it make?"

Rich shook his head. "You're Secret Service, aren't you? For some reason you thought Darrow was a threat even before all this."

"You've got a bright kid there, John," said Chuck.

"But the Secret Service," said Jade, "don't they just protect the President?"

"Two smart kids," said Kate.

Dad was nodding. "Which means?" he prompted them quietly.

"Nine hours," Jade realised. "The President of the United States is arriving *here* in nine hours?"

"To show support for the elections. He won't back off, he won't change his plans," Chuck told them. "If he cancels now and the press gets wind of it, it'll look like he's abandoning King Hassan, and the elections will lose all credibility. And if we announce that there's a problem and explain what it is, well, that's as good as surrendering to Prince Ali's faction."

"Which means," said Kate, "that we have a maximum of nine hours to find a nuclear bomb the size of a small briefcase on an airbase with several hundred buildings and 3,000 personnel. Or else we risk the President getting blown up with then rest of us."

17

The argument was inevitable, as was the outcome. Neither Jade nor Rich was willing to leave. They both insisted on staying to help look for the bomb.

Chance tried reasoning with them, he tried appealing to them, and he tried yelling at them. Nothing worked.

Finally Jade said to him, "Are *you* leaving?"

"What?"

"Are you leaving, and going somewhere safe? Or are you staying here on the base to look for the bomb?"

"I'm staying," Chance admitted.

"Fine. Then so are we," Jade told him.

"That's not an option."

"An option is a choice," said Rich. "And we're

choosing to stay. Look," he went on quickly, "why are you staying?"

"Because we have to find that bomb," Chance told him, "and the more people who are looking, the more chance we have of…" He stopped and sighed as he realised he was beaten.

"We'd better stay and help then," said Rich.

"Rather than arguing about this," added Jade, "let's just do it."

Two hours later, Rich was getting frustrated and nervous. He and Jade had been assigned a part of the living areas to search. There wasn't time for a full sweep, so their job was to knock on the doors of rooms in the barracks where the US airmen lived.

If anyone was in, they showed Darrow's photograph and asked if they'd seen him or anyone else unfamiliar in the last twenty-four hours. If there was no answer, Rich and Jade checked for signs of entry. If there were none, then they noted the address and a team would use a master key to gain access and do a check later.

If there were signs of a forced entry, then Rich and Jade were to find the nearest phone and call in immediately for a back-up team.

To get through the rooms quicker, they split up and worked independently, but it was a thankless and fruitless task, ticking off each room on a list as they checked it. Then they moved on to the next accommodation block.

It was Jade who spotted him. To Rich, it was just a distant figure – another US airman walking across the end of one of the runways. It looked like he'd just come from the main hangers and was on his way back to the main gates.

"That's him!" said Jade. "It's Darrow."

"You can't tell from this distance," Rich told her.

"I can. I spent enough time with that creep, and it's definitely him. Look at the way he walks, the way he's looking round to check no one's watching."

"Maybe." Rich wasn't convinced.

"I'm sure it is. Keep an eye on him. Don't let him out of your sight."

"Why? Where are you going?"

"I'm going to find Dad or Ardman or someone," said Jade.

"Or a phone."

"We call in, and they'll just think I'm a silly girl who's jumping to conclusions."

"Well..."

"See!" she exclaimed. "You think so too!"

Rich looked at his sister. Sure, she could be annoying, but one thing she *wasn't* was a silly girl who jumped to conclusions. He nodded. "If you're so sure, why do I have to watch him? Why can't I go for help and do the cavalry bit and be a hero?"

Jade sighed. "Because I saw him and if I'm wrong I'll take the heat. And more important, I'm faster than you."

Rich couldn't argue with that. "OK. Be as quick as you can, and I'll keep tabs on him."

"Just don't let him see you," Jade warned.

"As if."

Rich watched the uniformed figure that Jade insisted was Darrow walk across the end of a runway. In a few moments he would disappear among a group of maintenance and storage buildings. Rich glanced back at Jade, about to tell her he'd follow the figure. But Jade was already running towards the main administration block.

It took Jade nearly ten minutes to find Ardman, who was deep in conversation with Dex about the possible options. A white board on the wall of the office had a possible evacuation schedule drawn up. There were various timings, some crossed out. But even from a glance, Jade saw that the quickest evacuation plan would still take three days.

"You're sure it was Darrow?" asked Ardman as soon as Jade finished speaking.

She was still trying to catch her breath from running. "Not certain," she gasped. "But pretty sure. Maybe eighty per cent."

"Good enough for me," said Halford. "You go; I'll slow you down with this damned leg. I'll call John and let him know."

They had barely left the building when a Jeep roared up beside them. Jade was surprised to see her dad at the wheel.

"Get in!" he yelled. "Dex tells me you've spotted Darrow."

"Maybe," said Jade, leaping into the back of the Jeep. She pointed. "That way."

"Where's Rich?" Chance called over his shoulder as accelerated across the airfield.

"Don't ask," said Ardman from the passenger seat.

"He's following Darrow," shouted Jade above the

noise of the engine. "So we don't lose him."

"You sent Rich after an SAS-trained psycho-killer?" Chance yelled back.

"He's only following him. I told him to stay out of sight and not do anything daft."

Ardman made a point of inspecting his fingernails.

"This is your brother we're talking about," Chance yelled back at Jade. "And you think he won't do anything daft?"

"What were we supposed to do – just let Darrow walk away? Rich will be all right."

"I hope so. If Darrow spots Rich, the poor guy's in big trouble!"

The Jeep bounced angrily across the edge of runway as Chance floored the accelerator.

Rich kept to the shadows at the side of the buildings. He'd managed to get close enough to the man he was following to see that it really could be Darrow.

"Nice one, Jade," he murmured as he followed the figure between two brick-built storehouses.

The man paused and looked back, but Rich managed to duck into a doorway. He waited a moment, then peered cautiously round the edge of the wall. He caught the man's profile as he turned away. His cap was pulled down low over his eyes and he was wearing sunglasses, but it was definitely Darrow.

The question was, Rich thought, did he have the bomb with him? Or had he already planted it? He didn't seem to be carrying anything, so he'd probably already left it somewhere.

Rich hoped Jade wouldn't be long. Once out from this mini-maze of buildings, they'd be on the main road off the base, just five minutes' walk from the main gate.

If Darrow had a fake pass that could get him into the base, he'd be able to get out too. Should Rich follow him off the base? Would he have a car parked by the gate somewhere, or an accomplice waiting outside? Maybe Prince Ali himself would be somewhere nearby, though more likely he was miles away – partly as an alibi, and partly to be well out of the blast area…

Turning all these things over in his mind, Rich rounded another corner into a narrow alley.

The alley was empty. There was no sign of Darrow.

Rich swore under his breath, and ran to the end of the alley. He looked one way, then the other. Still no sign of Darrow. In fact, there was no sign of anyone. Just another narrow passage between two red brick buildings.

How could that happen? Rich was turning in bewilderment. He checked both ways again. The distance was just too great. There was no way that Darrow could have sprinted to the end of the passage that fast. The walls were flat and unbroken – no doorways or even windows.

It was just impossible. There was nowhere at all to hide, even if Darrow had spotted he was being followed. The passageway was only about a metre and a half wide. If Rich spread his arms, they'd touch the sides. He could probably brace himself between the two walls and climb up between them.

"Oh…" Rich felt suddenly cold as the possibility occurred to him.

He looked up.

Just in time to see Darrow braced between the two walls above his head. Just in time to see Darrow pull his feet away from one wall and drop towards Rich with the force of a sledgehammer.

The boy let out a yell of surprise as Darrow dropped

towards him. But Darrow wasn't worried. He'd just have to make this quick, in case anyone had heard. The boy was quick and he was resourceful – Darrow knew that from experience. And he mustn't forget this was John Chance's son.

For old times' sake, then, Darrow decided he might let the boy live. All he needed was a few minutes to get away.

The boy leaped aside as Darrow fell, but Darrow's boot crunched into his shoulder and sent him sprawling. He tried to get up, but Darrow was already on him. Darrow drew back his fist, but the constricted space was a disadvantage now and he couldn't get a good swing. His elbow jarred painfully on the brickwork, and the blow landed on the boy's chest.

It was enough to knock him down again and Darrow leaped at the kid, pinning him down with his knee as he prepared for the final punch. The kid was wriggling and fighting, and Darrow's next punch missed altogether, slamming into the concrete paving and painfully grazing his knuckles.

"Hold still!" said Darrow.

But the kid rolled violently the other way, sending Darrow pitching sideways. He was off balance as the kid kicked out, knocking him over. Darrow's cap and sunglasses fell to the ground.

Still, Darrow wasn't too worried. He was stronger, heavier, faster. He leaped back to his feet, turning to face the boy.

A fist slammed into Darrow's jaw. It surprised him more than hurt him. Then the boy lowered his head and charged. His shoulder caught Darrow in the stomach and sent him reeling, but he held on to the boy, dragging him down with him.

Somehow the boy was behind Darrow now, pinning him down with his knee jammed in his back. That was a mistake. Darrow grinned, knowing the kid couldn't see his face, and would have no warning as he prepared to heave himself upwards and throw the kidhim off. He imagined the boy slamming into the brick wall, maybe cracking his skull against it. Darrow braced himself.

Then everything changed.

Something cold and metallic jammed painfully into Darrow's cheek. He tried to turn to see what it was, but the boy grabbed his short hair.

"Hold still, or I'll blow your head off."

He sounded serious. But there was no way... Was

there? The cold metal dug into Darrow's skin – a gun?

"Don't be stupid," said Darrow, keeping his voice calm. "They'd never trust a kid like you with a gun."

"Want to bet?"

Darrow laughed. He braced himself. It was a good bluff, but now Rich would pay for it big time.

Then he heard the unmistakeable click-clack sound of a gun being cocked, right by his ear.

Darrow froze.

Jade was out of the Jeep before it stopped moving.

"He was heading for those buildings," she said.

"The main gate is just beyond, it's a short cut," Ardman told her. "Unless Rich managed to slow him down somehow we may be too late."

"They'll stop him at the gate," said Chance. "I hope."

"*If* they recognise him," said Ardman. He didn't sound optimistic.

Then they all heard the shout of surprise and fear from ahead of them.

"That was Rich!" Jade was sprinting for the buildings.

There was a narrow alley between them. She was

sure the cry had come from there. She raced along, guessing each turn as she sprinted through the warren of alleys and passages. Finally, she turned into a passageway and skidded to a halt in surprise.

Chance and Ardman were close behind. They, too, stopped as they took in the scene in front of them.

Darrow was lying face down on the ground. Rich was holding the stainless steel ballpoint pen he'd been using to mark their progress in the search of the rooms. He had the blunt end of it pressed hard into Darrow's cheek.

In his other hand he was holding the metal beetle he'd won on the Hook-a-Duck game at *Boscombe Heights*. The one that made the annoying click-clack noise.

"Like I said," Chance told them, "the poor guy's in big trouble." He walked slowly over to where Darrow was lying and drew a pistol from inside his jacket. "And believe me, Darrow, your trouble's only just beginning."

18

Darrow wasn't talking, but from the air tickets in his jacket pocket, Ardman knew they had till at least four o'clock that afternoon before the bomb was due to go off. The main airport wasn't far from the US base and Darrow would want to be well away before the explosion. The tickets, Ardman was amused to see, were booked in the name of Hilary Ardman.

It didn't give them much time. The bomb might be set to explode soon after Darrow's flight departed, but chances were he'd left a margin of error in case the flight was delayed. They might even have until the next day, but it was dangerous to make that sort of assumption. Whatever the case, they had a slight breathing space in which to get Darrow to tell them where he'd hidden the bomb.

Except that Darrow wasn't telling.

"Can't you just make him?" asked Rich on the flight back to the desert palace.

The isolated location, now securely in the control of Goddard's team, was the safest and best place to interrogate the prisoner and make sure he wouldn't be rescued. Prince Ali might have entire army units loyal to him, ready to move.

Rich and Jade were sitting opposite Chance and Ardman on a small, fast jet. Goddard was due to meet them from the landing strip near the palace, and Goddard would meet them there. Darrow was already on his way by helicopter, under careful guard courtesy of Chuck White's Secret Service team.

"*Make* him talk? Oh right," said Jade. "So, we're into torture now are we? Remind me – who are the terrorists here?"

"Well, if it's that or let tens of thousands of people get blown up…" Rich protested.

Chance watched them argue. "It isn't that simple, sadly," he said. "Darrow's been trained to hold out, and that's all he has to do. He has the luxury of time and we don't."

Ardman was talking quietly, but urgently, on a mobile phone. He ended the call and snapped the phone closed. "That's settled," he said, with the faintest trace of a smile.

"What?" Rich asked.

"The Professor is already on his way to join us on the fastest plane the RAF can spare. He agrees that Darrow can't be forced to talk, and he won't easily be tricked. But the Professor does have an interesting suggestion."

Jade had met the Professor before. With his dark beard and saturnine features, he looked like he had escaped from the ranks of Mephistopheles' henchmen. But he was actually a stage magician who specialised in mind-reading. Jade had seen him trick a gunman into telling them exactly what they wanted, and he'd told Jade some things about herself that she had no idea how he knew...

"So what's the Professor say we need to do?" she asked.

"Well, as I say, it's an interesting one," said Ardman. "The Professor suggests that we should let the bomb go off."

The Professor had already arrived by the time they got to the desert palace. A tall man in a dark suit, he was supervising several of Goddard's team. They seemed to be carrying buckets of rubble through to one of the rooms.

"We'll keep it round the corner here," the Professor told them. "Then it's ready to spread round as we need it. Thank you."

He smiled as he saw Jade. "It's Miss Chance. How delightful to see you again."

Jade grinned back at him and introduced Rich. The Professor shook his hand.

"You got everything you need?" asked Ardman.

"Almost. I think the RAF left my stomach behind somewhere over Kent. But apart from that…" He led Ardman through to one of the large reception rooms. "I've chosen this room as most suitable. You're sure the owner won't mind if we mess the place up a bit?" He sniffed. "Not that you'd notice actually, I think someone else got here before me. John Chance by the look of it." He turned to smile at Chance.

"Let's leave them to it," said Chance. "I want to check on Darrow."

"So what's this Professor bloke up to?" Rich wondered.

"Who knows? It'll be complicated and brilliant, though. Let's just hope it's brilliant enough to work on Darrow."

Watching on a monitor with Pete and Alan in the lab, it was soon clear that Darrow wasn't going to give away any information willingly.

The lab had been converted into an operations room like the one at Algernon's mansion house in England. Rich and Jade were surprised and pleased to find Dex Halford helping Pete set things up. Alan was busy at another computer.

Halford turned down the sound on the monitor showing Chance talking to Darrow. One of the SAS team who had stormed the palace stood in the corner of the small room. Still in his black uniform, he was holding an assault rifle and was obviously ready to step in if Darrow caused any trouble.

"You think Darrow will talk?" asked Rich.

"Not a hope," said Halford.

"So what's the Professor planning this time?" Jade wondered.

"I don't know, but he wants us to set up a video conference link with some number in the Greater

London area. Near Ealing. Guy called Mike."

Rich was interested in the technical stuff, but it left Jade cold. She left them to it. She was tired and thirsty, but it wasn't easy to relax knowing that a nuclear bomb might go off at any moment.

The Professor was talking with a group of people in the corridor outside the room he'd shown Ardman.

"We don't have time for a full rig," the Professor was saying. "Ideally we'd build a raised floor and false walls, but time is rather of the essence."

"How about we blow the supporting beams?" someone asked.

"Won't the floor just drop out?" someone else said. "Mind you, that'd be pretty convincing."

"Well, we don't blow them all, then. Just enough for the floor to shake."

The Professor nodded. "Could we do the same with the walls, do you think? Charges on the other side, enough to shake some plaster off?"

"Don't see why not," the man who'd talked about the floor beams said. "Easy enough, and pretty quick."

"Then that's what we do. And make sure there are no clocks in there."

Jade watched the men working furiously for a few

more minutes – rigging the furniture in the room with tiny detonators, and fixing devices on the adjoining walls. When she went downstairs, she found a team in the room below attaching putty-like plastic explosive to exact points marked on the ceiling. She had little doubt that something similar must be happening on the floor of the room above the Professor as well, but she had no idea why.

They were all still hard at work when she returned from the kitchens with a pot of coffee and tray of mugs to take down to Rich and the others in the lab.

Ardman was rubbing his hands together and looking pleased as Jade passed. He was deep in conversation with the Professor.

"We've taken his watch along with his belt and other possessions. Oh, and we've slipped a little something into his tea," said the Professor, catching sight of Jade and the tray. "Just enough to disorient him slightly and with luck it'll put him to sleep. In this heat he has to drink something, even if he thinks we may have drugged it. But he seems fairly relaxed. When we wake him, he'll have no idea how long he's been out."

"Everything else on track?" asked Ardman.

"I was just going to check with Pete whether he'd

got Mike online yet. I'd like to know how the plate work is going." The Professor turned to Jade as she passed. "I hope you've got a spare mug here for me."

In the lab, Pete was talking to a man with long, dark hair on one of the monitor screens.

"I've found a local news crew who are getting me the plate shots," the man was saying. He grinned as he saw the Professor appear beside Pete on his own monitor. "Hi, Guv. How's it going?"

"Hello, Mike," said the Professor. "We're all set at our end. Just waiting for you."

"Shouldn't be a problem. I've got the elements coming together. As I was saying, the news crew can give me good enough backgrounds, and I'll degrade them anyway to look like mobile phone footage or amateur stuff. Have you thought about EMP, by the way?"

The Professor sighed and muttered something under his breath. Jade looked at Rich, who just shrugged as if to say, "Don't ask me."

"Good point," said the Professor. "Let's just hope he doesn't think of that."

"We'll go to static or something at the end anyway. That might be enough."

The Professor nodded. "We're going to let him sleep

for a bit, but time is getting tight. How long do you need?"

"Longer than we've got. I found some footage of the local hospital with ambulances and stuff. Got an actor friend to do a voice-over, which he thinks is for a demo-reel. Which it might be actually, if I can show it to prospective clients once you're done with it. I could do with the work. Give me an hour and I'll stream it over to Pete to sort out."

The Professor thanked Mike, and Pete ended the call.

"We're all set," said Pete. "Got a cable link to the room. So long as your explosives guys don't cut the link or blow up the TV by mistake we'll be fine."

"Excellent." The Professor clapped his hands together. "Just time for a mug of coffee then, thank you, Jade. Then we'll blow everything up."

There was an anxious but expectant hush in the laboratory. Rich and Jade were sitting at the back of the group watching the main screen. They had to crane their necks to see over Ardman, Halford, the Professor, Pete and Alan and several other people including Goddard.

The wide screen showed a good view of the room the Professor's team had been working on. There was a large wooden desk, with leather captain's chairs either side. A large LCD television was on one wall, a painting of a ship at sea on another. A glittering chandelier hung from the ceiling.

As they watched, the door opened and John Chance led Darrow into the room. He gestured for Darrow to sit one side of the desk while he sat the other. The SAS guard closed the door and stood in front of it.

"So why the change of scene?" asked Darrow. He leaned back in the chair, looking totally relaxed.

"I thought maybe after your long sleep, you might be more amenable."

"Ah, thumbscrews time, is it?"

"Quite the opposite. I'm authorised to make you an offer."

Darrow laughed. "I wasn't asleep that long, and I wasn't born yesterday."

"You were asleep for hours," said Chance. There was a fleeting look of surprise on Darrow's face, but Chance went on quickly: "And you might not have been born yesterday, but you let a kid with a biro get the better of you yesterday."

"Yesterday?"

Chance ignored him. "So, how much do you want? Be realistic, and you can walk out of here very rich. Just tell us where the bomb is hidden."

For a moment, Rich thought Darrow was going to do it, but then he grinned. "No chance. Or maybe that should be no, Mr Chance." He laughed. "When that bomb goes off, I'll be richer than you can imagine. And Ali won't let you keep me. Once he's in control you'll have to hand me over. We're still in East Araby and I'm guessing time is getting a bit tight now. Too late to get me out of the country, I'll bet."

Chance's fist slammed down on to the desk. "Damn it, Darrow – just tell us. Have you any idea how many people will die if you don't?"

Darrow seemed unfazed. "Pretty good one, yes. And you know what? I don't care."

Chance leaned back in his chair as if defeated. "That's it then. I can't help you. You'll be flown back to the airfield, where we're going to hand you over to King Hassan's security people. Just pray the bomb gets you before they start work on you."

Darrow laughed again, though this time it sounded forced. "That lot? They're amateurs. And the King doesn't have the stomach to let them do a proper job anyway. Plus they'll know the score, and they know their own fate lies with Ali. They'll want to keep in his good books no matter what."

"We'll see." Chance stood up.

In front of Rich, the Professor was speaking quietly into a mobile phone. "Yes please, now," Rich heard him say.

A moment later there was the sound of someone knocking on a door. The SAS guard opened the door and took a note from the person outside. Without comment, he walked across and handed it to Chance, who read it.

"He'll be expecting us to try something," the Professor explained. "So we will. And you never know he might even fall for it. Though that will make us look a bit silly after all our other efforts."

Chance looked up. "Well, it's academic now. You missed your opportunity. And I think King Hassan's people will actually be very pleased to see you."

"What do you mean?" asked Darrow suspiciously.

"We've found the bomb."

There was silence for several seconds. Then Chance went on, "Turns out it wasn't that well hidden at all, was it. You obviously didn't expect anyone to go looking for it. You didn't know we'd found out the bomb existed or maybe you'd have done a better job of hiding it. The Secret Service has a Nuclear Containment Team on site. They've already made it safe."

"It was hidden well enough," said Darrow. Was it just the image on the screen, Rich wondered, or did the man look pale?

"You call that well hidden? A child could have found it. Probably it was a child who did find it – like one who got the better of you."

Darrow tilted his head slightly to one side. Then he nodded and very slowly started to clap his hands. "Very good. And this is the bit where I say something like 'Gosh, and I never thought you'd look in the base commander's waste bin,' is it?" He shook his head and laughed. "Oldest trick in the book."

Chance stood up again. "Well, we had to try," he admitted.

In the laboratory, Ardman tapped Alan on the shoulder. "Have them check the base commander's waste bin anyway," he said. "Just in case. Mr Darrow does have rather a warped sense of humour."

Alan nodded and reached for a phone.

"And do you think now is the moment?" Ardman asked the Professor.

"As good a time as any," the Professor said. He stood up and loosened his tie. "I'll just prepare for my big moment. Yes please, Pete – whenever you're ready."

"My pleasure," Pete said. He pulled a keyboard towards him. "Three, two, one, zero." As he finished speaking, he pressed the Enter key.

And the whole building shook, as if it had been hit by a nuclear blast. A moment later, there was a colossal *boom*.

19

The whole room shuddered. Plaster fell from the walls. The glass beads of the chandelier were jangling together. The painting fell, frame splitting as it hit the floor. Darrow's chair shook so much it looked like it might fall apart. One leg of the desk collapsed, papers sliding across the surface as the whole thing tipped.

"Is it that time already?" said Darrow as the sound and the vibration subsided.

Chance stared open-mouthed at him.

"You inhuman monster," he finally spat out. "You actually let it happen!" He looked as if he was about to reach across the desk and haul Darrow bodily from his chair, but at that moment the door opened and the Professor hurried in past the SAS guard. His shirt was untucked and his tie was at an angle. His face was smeared with dirt. There was plaster dust stuck in his dark beard. The corridor outside was strewn with rubble.

"Oh my God," the Professor. "So many people… It's all over the news."

Chance grabbed a remote control from the desk and turned on the TV mounted on the wall. The picture was breaking up, the sound distorted, but it showed the scene at the capital.

The distinctive skyline of East Araby's capital city was ragged and torn. Behind it, from the direction of the US airbase, a huge mushroom cloud was rising into the dusty sky. The footage was shaky and low-definition. The BBC World News banner was splashed across the bottom of the screen.

"We're just getting these images from our reporter's mobile phone," the announcer was saying. "It certainly looks like a major incident. We can switch now to live coverage from the East Araby News Network."

The picture broke up, and when it reformed again it showed ambulances and fire engines speeding along a highway. Again, in the background, the mushroom cloud continued to billow upwards into the sky.

"We don't have sound," the announcer said, "but obviously the East Araby authorities are mobilising all their emergency services. We are still waiting for news of whether Air Force One had left East Araby or if the President is still in the city. There is also no news yet of King Hassan, though Crown Prince Ali has announced he will be making an official statement shortly."

The picture cut back to more mobile phone footage of the explosion. The image held for a few moments, then broke up into static and white noise.

Chance turned off the television and hurled the remote control away.

"What have you done?" he hissed at Darrow. "How many have you killed?"

"I'm just the messenger," said Darrow. He sounded as smug as ever, but he was looking shaken.

"How can you just sit there?" the Professor said. "We had people on that base, and in the city. Good people. Never mind the thousands of civilians." He suddenly grabbed Darrow by the front of his shirt and hauled him to his feet. "And you just sit there!"

Darrow tried to shake free, but the Professor was pushing him back down into the chair anyway. "You didn't even have the decency to hit a military target, did you?" he shouted.

"What do you mean?"

"You saw where that cloud was."

"It was the airbase," said Chance. "Has to be."

"You think so? Because I don't. He didn't even dare go to the base, did he?"

"That is where we found him," said Chance.

"A decoy then!" The Professor was ranting now, breathing heavily and clenching his fists. "That cloud was over the residential area. The hospital, schools, children's playgrounds. That was your target wasn't it?!" He grabbed Darrow again and pushed him to the ground. "You piece of dirt! Is that all you're good for – killing the sick and the kids? Is it?!"

"The bomb was on the base," Darrow told him, wiping a smear of blood from his mouth. "That was the point."

"Never! We'd have found it. You knew that, you couldn't take the risk. You weren't man enough. So where did you leave it? A litter bin in the park, was it?"

The Professor advanced threateningly at Darrow, who was still lying on the floor. He pushed himself backwards, watching the man warily. "It was on the base," he repeated.

"A school canteen, maybe?"

"On the base."

"Under some old woman's bed in the hospital? I bet that was it." He took a swift step towards Darrow, drawing his leg back to kick him hard.

"It was on the airbase!"

"No. You couldn't hide it from us. You're not clever enough, for that – not for anything more than blowing up little kids and old women. We searched every inch of that base, and it wasn't there. So where was it? Hospital? School? Bus station?"

"On the base," insisted Darrow. "In one of the hangers. You'll know soon enough."

"No we won't, because we searched the hangers. It was in the school, wasn't it? The nursery school three blocks from the base."

"In the hanger."

"Liar!" The Professor pulled out a handgun and trained it on Darrow, his hand shaking. "You'll die a liar and a coward."

"It was in the hanger, where you'd never find it."

The shot ripped into the marble floor close to

Darrow's head. "We'd have found it!"

"Not inside the engine housing of a B-2 Stealth Bomber, you wouldn't!"

The Professor froze, suddenly incredibly calm. "No," he said quietly. "We probably wouldn't." He turned to Chance. "I reckon that was about two minutes, don't you?"

"Not bad," agreed Chance.

Darrow stared up at them, the confusion on his face gradually giving way to fury. He leaped to his feet and hurled himself at the Professor.

The Professor didn't move or blink. He just let the SAS man from the doorway hammer his shoulder into Darrow and send him sprawling.

"You know," said the Professor. "I did worry you might realise about the EMP. But it seems you're not as good as we feared after all. A bit pathetic really." Then he turned away, and he and Chance left the room.

Ardman put down his phone. "Chuck White has passed that on to the Nuclear Containment Team. So, problem solved – hopefully."

"We still need to round up Crown Prince Ali and his cohorts," said Halford.

"Shouldn't be too tricky now their plan has failed. And King Hassan will have the evidence he needs to move openly against them. Prince Ali can't play the popularity card after it gets out that he was willing to murder thousands of his own people. I imagine his military support is already evaporating."

The Professor and John Chance arrived, obviously pleased with how things had gone.

"I wasn't sure he would tell us," admitted Chance, "but the news footage was pretty convincing."

"Oh, Mike knows his stuff. Even in a hurry, he's the best."

"Who *is* this Mike guy?" asked Jade.

"He works in the film industry," the Professor explained. "Film and TV, actually. He has a small company that does special effects. They make models, fly spaceships, recreate historic events and natural disasters, blow things up – as you saw. That was a combination of video footage, of the real airbase and city, with some computer animation and digital painting for the damaged buildings added and a film of a controlled explosion Mike arranged. A much smaller explosion than it looked, obviously, but when it's combined with the other visual elements, then degraded to look like it was shot on a mobile phone… Combine that with shaking the room and knocking a bit of plaster off the walls and ceiling and, well, the effect is quite startling."

"It convinced me," Rich agreed. "And I *knew* it was all a fake."

"We did worry he'd work it out," said Chance.

"EMP," said Rich.

The Professor smiled. "Exactly."

He and Chance went to talk to Ardman, leaving Jade and Rich alone at the back of the lab.

"So what's this EMP thing?" Jade asked Rich.

"I didn't realise before. It's an Electro-Magnetic Pulse. When a nuclear bomb goes off, it knocks out all the electronic equipment in the area."

Jade nodded. "So the news camera and mobile phone shouldn't have been working."

"That's right."

"Lucky Darrow didn't spot that."

"Lucky should be our middle name," said Rich. As he spoke, he glanced at the main screen set up on one of the lab workbenches.

"What is it?" Jade asked, seeing his expression. She turned to look.

The screen was still showing the room where their father had interrogated Darrow, and where the SAS man should have been keeping Darrow under guard. The heavy door was locked from the outside, so even if Darrow somehow managed to immobilise the guard there was absolutely no way he could get out.

Until now.

"Oh my God," said Rich. "Not so lucky."

He and Jade ran for the door, shouting urgently to Chance.

Darrow was beaten. He knew there was no way he could hope to overpower the guard, and that even if he *did* he couldn't go anywhere. He could try to shoot out the lock on the door, but there would be other guards outside. His choice was between going out in a blaze of glory, or waiting to see what justice had to offer.

Maybe he could force them to repatriate him to Britain and serve a prison sentence there. But more likely the Americans would want him and he would disappear for ever into some prison camp that didn't officially exist. But even that was preferable to facing trial – or *not* facing trial – in East Araby.

Then fate played its hand, and suddenly Darrow's options were very different.

The floor was covered with heavy, marble tiles. Crown Prince Ali had demanded nothing but the very best from his builders. The floor was specially reinforced so it could take the tremendous weight of the marble.

But that was before the Professor's team had blown out some of the joists to make the room shake as if caught at the edge of a nuclear blast.

The first clue Darrow had that something was wrong was when the floor shifted slightly under his feet. He glanced at the SAS man standing by the door. Close to the wall, the effect was less noticeable and the guard just stared back at Darrow.

Trying to look casual, Darrow slumped down as heavily as he could in the nearest chair. Again he felt the floor move. More marked now, the guard seemed to have realised something was amiss. Darrow knew he had to act quickly.

He jumped to his feet, making a point of stretching and groaning as if sore from his exertions. He then leaned forward and rested his hands on the edge of the heavy wooden desk. It rocked slightly as he put his weight on it, one of the legs having been blown off earlier.

Then, with an almighty effort, Darrow gripped the side of the desk and heaved. The desk lifted, turned, toppled, and Darrow leaped backwards. The guard gave a shout of surprise and stepped forward.

But it was too late. The weight of the desk hitting the weakened floor was enough to break through the remaining, damaged floor supports. The centre of the room collapsed. Marble tiles slid and fell. The desk crashed through to the room below leaving a ragged hole.

The guard staggered forwards, off balance as the floor tilted and bucked. Darrow paused only to kick viciously at the man and knock him down. Then, grabbing the guard's assault rifle, he leaped into the hole left by the desk.

Moments later, the door crashed open and Chance ran in. He skidded to a halt, almost losing his balance on the broken floor. Rich and Jade were close behind him. Chance held out his arms to keep them back, as a burst of automatic fire hammered through the hole in the floor and shattered the chandelier.

In the room below, Darrow landed painfully on a pile of rubble. His ankle twisted under him, but he ignored the pain. He let off a burst of gunfire in case the guard had recovered and was trying to follow him. Then he hurried to the door, out into the corridor, and he was running for the stairs, ignoring the pain in his ankle. He knew the layout of the desert palace from several visits, and he knew the only ways out were the airstrip – too far away – and the helicopter pad on the roof.

Whatever Chance and Ardman and their colleagues thought, Darrow still had a job to do…

20

The limousine was cool and quiet. After the frantic activity of the previous day, Rich was glad of the calm. He sat beside Dex, facing Jade and Chance.

The elation at having found – and made safe – the nuclear bomb was tinged with annoyance that Darrow had managed to get away. But Rich was determined that he wasn't going to let that get him down. Let Darrow fly off into the sunset in his stolen helicopter. Dad said he was a survivor, and that he'd steer well clear of them and keep his head down from now on. Not least as Crown Prince Ali and his supporters would also be looking for Darrow after he'd let them down.

It was strange, but Rich was more nervous about

what lay ahead than he had been about anything else. He felt uncomfortable and out of place in the smart white suit Ardman had arranged. It didn't help that his father and Halford both looked completely at ease in theirs, as if being invited to meet a king and a president were business as usual for them.

He guessed Jade must be nervous, but she didn't show it. She looked stunning in a pale blue dress that ended below her knees.

Ardman had laughed when Rich asked if he was invited. "How can I be invited?" he had said. "I don't exist." More seriously, he'd pointed out that it was essential that no one know what had happened. If other security forces spotted him at a reception with King Hassan and the US President, they might well guess that there had been a problem. At this key moment – the week before the elections – King Hassan wanted no hint of anything awry.

"So how come Dad's going?" Jade had asked.

"Oh, we're old friends, the President and me," replied Chance. Neither Rich nor Jade could tell if he was joking.

The limo pulled into the gates of the King's impressive Pearl Palace. They waited while heavily armed soldiers checked the driver's papers. Rich turned to look out of the window. Even through the darkened glass, he could see that the huge palace walls almost glowed in the sunlight, which was how it had got its name. High towers rose above the main palace.

They were escorted through a huge hallway lined with statues and vases filled with impressive arrangements of flowers, and out into a central courtyard. A fountain stood in the middle of a large ornamental pond. Small trees round the pond gave welcome shade. At one end of the courtyard was a covered area over a dais with a red carpet.

"Guess that's where it all happens, then," said Rich. He had managed to get a disposable camera from the reception at their hotel. "Think they'll let me take some pictures?" He took out the camera and lined up the podium through the view finder.

"No," said Chance. He lifted the camera from Rich's grasp and put it in his own jacket pocket. "I don't."

Rich sniffed with annoyance. "They can't stop me eating peppermints though, can they?" He had a tube of mints in his other pocket and offered them round.

Halford laughed and accepted one. Chance shook his head sadly.

Jade glared. "Honestly!"

"What?" asked Rich, popping a mint in his mouth. "This girl I met on a roller coaster had some, they're good. You should try one."

"Sometimes I cannot believe you are my brother." Jade took the tube of mints from him and stuffed them into her small clutch bag.

"At least I'm looking smart," Rich told her. He braced himself for a punch, but Jade smiled.

"You reckon?" she said.

There were other guests already in the large courtyard, and more were arriving all the time. Waiters with trays of orange juice and sparkling water moved among the gathering crowd.

Rich recognised a broad-shouldered man in a dark suit wearing sunglasses and pointed him out. "Look, there's Chuck White. Offer him one of those mints, Jade, he likes them."

Jade rolled her eyes.

Halford went over to talk briefly to the Secret Service man. Rich looked round for Kate Hunter, but he couldn't see her. Maybe she was with the President and King Hassan, wherever they were.

"Hey," said Jade, pointing across to the other side of

the pond, "that's Crown Prince Ali. What's he doing here?"

"Not sure he's here through choice," said Chance. "Notice how those two men are standing very close to him?"

"That's right," said Halford, rejoining them. "He's effectively under arrest, but King Hassan doesn't want to announce it until after the elections. Thinks it might look like he's trying to influence the outcome or subdue opposition. The President agrees, so Chuck tells me. They want it all smooth as a baby's bottom."

"Let's hope they're careful," said Chance. "They might be smooth, but babies' bottoms can do some rather unpleasant things."

"I still don't really get how it was supposed to work," admitted Rich, sipping at his orange juice. "I mean, surely blowing up half the capital would just make people want elections more, not less."

"I think Price Ali was planning that the military would then take over and he'd be able to assume control."

"So what was to stop King Hassan just going on TV and telling everyone what really happened?" Jade asked. "Once their plot was discovered, why didn't they just back off? Or don't the people trust their King?"

"Oh, they love him," said Halford. "That's why he can get away with the US connection, and have elections without fear of other states in the area getting upset with him. My guess is that they were hoping King Hassan would be killed in the blast."

"Makes sense," Chance agreed. "In fact, for their plan to be sure of success, Crown Prince Ali would have had to be in control. With Hassan dead, he'd become king. It's lucky they needed the nuclear explosion as an excuse to cut their ties with the US, or else they could just have assassinated the King. But enough of all that. We're here to enjoy ourselves, right?"

"Right!" agreed Jade.

In among the dignitaries and the diplomats, the rich and the influential, Rich thought that Jade looked at home. They really should be making the most of it, he thought. They were about to meet the US President. It was a glorious, sunny day, but somehow, something wasn't right. He could feel it. He could almost, but not quite, tell what it was.

"What's wrong?" asked Jade, seeing Rich's perplexed expression.

"I don't know. Nothing. King Hassan was here yesterday, wasn't he? Ready to meet the President."

"That's right," agreed Halford. "The President came here straight from the air field, as soon as he arrived."

"But this palace is right over the other side of the capital," Rich realised. "There's no way the blast would have killed King Hassan."

"So?" asked Jade. Then she realised. "But they needed the King dead. We just said that."

Halford was looking over towards the dais. "Here comes the King now, and the President."

"Then you'd better find your friend Chuck," Chance told him. "Because Jade's right. They must have planned an assassination as well. Then Ali could cancel the elections and throw out the Americans; Hassan never would – even with the blast."

"You don't think…?" Halford's voice tailed off.

"And now the bomb plot has failed, they'll need a very public, high-profile disaster instead. One that involves the Americans too. Something that can be blamed on them, at least superficially."

"Like what?" asked Rich. But really, he already knew.

"Like King Hassan being caught in the crossfire when the American President is assassinated."

Halford was hurrying towards the dais, but everyone else was moving that way too. The President and the King were shaking hands with people, laughing and joking, making their way slowly towards the podium to giver their speeches – two leaders expressing mutual support and admiration.

John Chance turned and hurried the other way.

Jade and Rich were immediately after him. "Where are we going?" asked Jade.

"If there's a bomb, then we have to leave it to Halford to get Chuck White's team on the case. If they see us searching, or trying to get people out, they'll detonate anyway. But if there's a sniper, which is more likely given the security here, then we have to find him quick."

Chance paused in an archway that led back into the main palace. "You get back to the reception. Play along, behave like nothing's wrong."

"And where are you going?" demanded Rich.

"If I were taking the shot, I'd be at the top of that." He pointed up at the tall tower above them.

"We're coming with you," said Jade.

"No time to argue about it," Rich told him.

Their father glared at them for moment, then turned and hurried into the palace.

There was a soldier standing at the bottom of a narrow flight of steps that led up the tower. He looked like an officer, in flat cap with a gun holstered at his side.

"Secret Service," Chance announced. "Just got to check up the tower."

The soldier nodded and stepped aside.

Then, suddenly, he drew the handgun from his holster and levelled it at Chance.

"Guess that confirms it, then," said Chance. "You go for help," he added, turning to Jade and Rich.

The soldier glanced at them too. He didn't take his eyes off Chance for more than a split second, but when he looked back, it was in time to see Chance's fist smash into his face. He collapsed silently to the ground. Chance took the gun from the soldier's hand and checked it was loaded.

"Well, go on," he said, before turning and running up the stairs.

"You go," said Jade to Rich. "I'm following Dad."

"No – you go," insisted Rich. "You're quicker, remember."

She sighed. "In this dress? Get real." Then she turned, and hurried up the steps after her father.

Rich shook his head in disbelief before running back to the courtyard.

By the time Jade arrived, it was almost over. One soldier was lying unconscious on the small roof of the tower. Her father was just punching another one hard in the stomach. The soldier doubled over, and Chance's knee crashed into his face.

A third soldier grabbed Chance from behind. Jade shouted a warning, but just too late. Chance tried to raise his handgun to fire a shot to warn the Secret Service in the courtyard below, but the soldier knocked the gun away. It skidded across the ground.

Even so, Chance managed to shake the man off. He spun round, thumping the soldier hard so he spun away towards the low wall round the roof. He slumped close to where a sniper rifle was set up on a tripod. It was fitted with a telescopic sight and pointing down between two parapets into the courtyard below.

The soldier struggled back to his feet, but Chance took three steps across the roof and kicked him hard. This time he stayed down.

Jade ran forward, but then a hand closed over her mouth and dragged her back. She could only watch wide-eyed as another figure stepped out from an alcove at the edge of the roof and picked up the fallen handgun.

Mark Darrow aimed the gun straight at Chance.

Chance backed away. "You can't shoot me. It'll warn the President's men."

"Might be worth it, though." He stepped forward and thumped the gun into Chance's head, clubbing him to the ground.

Jade tore free of the soldier holding her and ran to help her father back to his feet.

"Losing your cool, Mark?" Chance asked as Jade helped him up.

"Just having fun." Darrow glanced over the parapet. "They'll talk for a while, I think. These politicians and rulers like the sound of their own voices. Now, quickly but carefully, empty your pockets."

"I'm travelling light," Chance told him. He took Rich's camera out of his jacket, held it for a moment as if surprised to find it there, then put it down on top of the parapet close to the rifle. He placed his wallet beside the camera, angled against the rising parapet.

Then he pulled a handful of loose change from his trouser pocket, and balanced it on top of the camera before stepping away.

"Now you," said Darrow to Jade.

"No pockets," she told him.

"Handbag, then."

"Just a clutch and peppermints." She took them out. "Want one?"

"No."

"I will," said Chance. He ignored Darrow's glare, took a mint from the offered pack, and popped it into his mouth.

"OK," said Darrow, "so you've made your little gesture. Now back away. It's show time."

Chance took Jade's clutch bag and placed it carefully beside the camera and his wallet. Then he took Jade's hand and together they backed away. From the back of the roof, they still had a good view between the parapets down into the courtyard. The President and King Hassan were just stepping on to the dais. The President waved to the assembled crowd.

Two of the four soldiers on the roof were still unconscious. The other two stood side by side with Jade and Chance, handguns levelled at them. Darrow took his place at the rifle, shouldering the butt and looking down through the telescopic sight.

"Ringside seats for you guys," he said, without turning from his position. "One false move, one sound of warning, and the Prince's Royal Guard will drop you where you stand. Got it?"

"Got it," said Jade. Her stomach was doing flip-flops as she watched Darrow take aim.

Down below, the President was stepping towards a microphone. King Hassan stood beside him. Crown Prince Ali was at the side of the dais. He seemed to glance up at the tower, knowing what was about to happen – what Jade and Chance were powerless to stop. There was no sign of Rich.

Suddenly there was movement at the side of the dais. Halford was pushing forward through the crowd. Chuck jumped up at the side of the platform.

Darrow's finger tightened on the trigger.

"You know," said Chance out loud, "this peppermint is *revolting*."

To Jade's amazement, he took the mint out of his mouth and flicked it away.

On the dais, Chuck hurled himself at the President,

but Prince Ali stepped forward, blocking his movement.

The President didn't seem to see. He was standing absolutely still as Darrow squeezed the trigger.

The bullet left Darrow's rifle at over three times the speed of sound and slammed into flesh and bone less than a second later, killing instantly.

21

Everything happened so fast that it took Jade a moment to work out what was going on.

Just as he saw Darrow exhale ready to take the shot, John Chance flicked his peppermint away. The mint rolled along the parapet close to the sniper rifle. It dropped over the side, bounced on to Chance's angled wallet and rolled across Jade's clutch bag.

Then it hit the coins balanced on top of Rich's camera. The tiny extra pressure was enough to set off the shutter – and trigger the automatic flash.

The sudden bright glare caught Darrow by surprise as he took the shot. It didn't disturb his aim by much. But it was enough.

Crown Prince Ali had stepped in between Chuck

White and the President. White was knocked aside, and the Crown Prince staggered sideways – right into the path of Darrow's misaimed bullet.

The Prince was hurled backwards, dead before he hit the floor.

Darrow had been ready to take out King Hassan after the President, but knowing he had missed, he hesitated.

With the two soldiers distracted by the camera flash and the events happening on the podium below, Chance moved swiftly. He kicked the legs out from under one of the men, and punched the other one hard enough to floor him.

Darrow turned at the commotion.

"You're finished," said Chance. "Give up now."

"I can still kill Hassan," said Darrow. "The Prince's faction will take control."

He turned back to the rifle, lifting it off the tripod and quickly taking aim. Down below there was pandemonium. Kate Hunter had appeared out of nowhere and was hustling the President off the dais, but Jade could see that Darrow still had a clear shot at the King.

But then something streaked past both Jade and

Chance and cannoned into Darrow. Rich was a rolling ball of arms and legs that sent Darrow flying. The rifle was knocked from his grasp and toppled over the parapet.

"Glad you could join us," said Chance.

But the good humour was short lived.

Darrow still had Chance's handgun. Jade launched herself at him, but he shoved her aside.

Rich and Chance both tensed, ready to leap at Darrow, but he had hold of Jade's arm and hauled her up – the gun pressed to her temple.

"You can't get away," Chance told Darrow.

"Watch me."

"You harm her…" Chance warned.

"I'm not going to harm her. She's my ticket out of here. Once I'm safely away then I'll let her go. Maybe," he added, as if it was an afterthought.

Jade was struggling. She tried to turn her head enough to bite Darrow's hand as he held her, but he was too strong, and he was ready for her. He wrenched her head hard against the gun.

"Don't even think about it," warned Darrow. "Now you and I are going to walk out of here. Very slowly and very calmly. He started to edge forwards, pushing

Jade with him. "Neat trick with the camera, by the way. Though it's been done before."

"That was for Ferdy," said Chance quietly. He was holding the handgun from one of the soldiers he'd floored and aimed it at Darrow. "Now, you hold it right there."

Darrow grinned suddenly. "I don't think you'd be that stupid. Not without a clear shot, and I won't give you that. Take one shot and you know what I'll do." He jabbed the gun harder into Jade's temple.

"Just let them go, Dad," said Rich. His voice was trembling. "You can't play games with Jade's life."

"He's right," said Darrow. "You know, Ferdy begged. Begged for his life. Are you going to beg, John? For the life of your daughter?"

"It's all right, Jade," said Chance. "We'll get you out of this safely. Just stay calm, OK?" Slowly, he lowered the gun.

Jade nodded, as best she could. The gun was against her temple, and Darrow was holding her upper arm tightly.

Jade could hear the sound of running feet on the stairs, but she knew that she had to act now. King Hassan's troops might open fire on the man who tried to kill their King and never mind who else got in the way.

"It's OK, Dad," she said. "I'm cool. Remember what I told you in the desert? Remember what I always say, and believe me – I mean it. Just – *chillax*."

"I remember," said Chance. In one fluid movement, he raised the gun and fired straight at the middle of Jade's forehead.

Rich watched Jade's fingers counting down as she spoke. Even so, he could not believe his father had really just shot at her.

At the same moment he fired, Jade lifted her feet off the ground, putting her entire weight on Darrow's arms. The sudden strain caught Darrow by surprise, and Jade dropped – not far, but far enough.

The bullet from Chance's handgun hammered into Darrow at exactly the point where Jade's forehead had just been – right in the middle of his chest. The power of the blow was enough to send him reeling backwards. His back caught on the lowest part of the parapet, and he flipped over it.

There was no cry of surprise or fear as Darrow fell. He was dead already.

Chuck White, sweating and pale, pounded up the last stairs and on to the roof in time to see Darrow fall.

"Guess you don't need the Cavalry after all," he said. "It seems like no matter what they say, we should always leave these things to Chance."

Like the nuclear explosion, it was all a trick. Jade watched the news on the TV in their hotel suite in amazement.

"How can they do this?"

All the guests had been cleared immediately from the palace after the shootings. Like everyone else, Chance, Halford, Rich and Jade had been bundled out and into their limousine. King Hassan's own Royal Guards were rounding up supporters of Crown Prince Ali, while the Secret Service made preparations for the President's immediate departure.

The TV news was cutting between footage of the crowds at the palace taken before the President and King Hassan arrived, and the speeches. Speeches that Jade knew had been made to an empty courtyard after everyone had left.

She laughed out loud as she heard first the President, then King Hassan pay tribute to the late

Crown Prince Ali who had – apparently – died saving his beloved nephew the King from an assassin's bullet.

"He threw himself in front of the shot!" Jade gasped. "Who are they kidding?"

"Maybe no one," agreed Chance, "but it's a way of getting Ali's supporters on his side. Their figurehead died a hero, and in doing so he endorsed the current leadership and by default endorsed its decision to hold an election. Pretty shrewd stuff."

"But it's all lies. It's dishonest."

Rich grinned. "It's politics. Anyway, it's no more dishonest than saying 'shoot me right here'," he tapped his forehead, "and then ducking away."

"Duck away from this," said Jade, and threw a cushion at him.

Rich caught it easily and threw it back.

"Doesn't it upset you, though?" asked Jade.

"Only thing that upsets me is I didn't get to meet the President after all," said Rich.

They were interrupted by a knock at the door. It was Ardman. He was carrying a large bunch of flowers and a bottle of champagne.

"These are for you," he said, handing the flowers to Jade. He gave the champagne to Chance. "And this is for you. Compliments of Mr White and Miss Hunter."

"Hey, I was there too, you know," Rich complained.

"Oh yes, sorry. Nearly forgot." Ardman took something from his pocket and handed it to Rich.

He looked at it dubiously. "So, Dad gets champagne and Jade gets a bouquet. And I get a disposable camera."

"I gather yours got knocked off a wall when Darrow fell."

"True," admitted Rich.

"Oh, and you get these too," said Ardman. He handed each of them a plain white envelope.

"What is this?" asked Chance.

Jade had already opened hers. "Hey – awesome!"

Rich was impressed too. "An invitation to a special reception at the White House?!"

"There will be other people there too, of course," said Ardman. "But the President is very keen for you three to be there. Mr White tells me the President was very sorry not to be able to meet you earlier today and wishes to make up for it." Ardman smiled. "I'll pay for the flights and hotels. Or rather, I'll suggest the Foreign Office charge King Hassan for it."

Chance coughed. "I, er, don't actually have much leave left."

Ardman nodded seriously. "I know. But since this is a special occasion I'm willing to let you have a few extra days."

"Yeah, Dad," said Rich. "You don't get out of it that easily."

"That's right, you have to be there too," Jade told him.

Chance laughed. "OK, no problem. Actually, I'm looking forward to it. It'll take a crisis bigger than the one we just sorted out to keep me away from making that reception. I'll definitely be there."

"Just so long as you two don't get into any trouble while you're there," added Ardman.

"We won't," said Rich.

"No way," agreed Jade.

Like their father, they were both going to be proved very wrong indeed.

Watch out for the Chance twins
in their next adventure,
First Strike - in bookstores
July 2009...

Don't miss the previous adventures of the Chance twins:

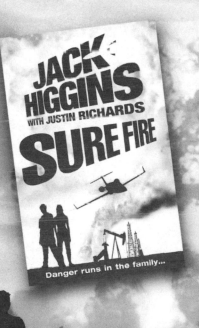